THE SURPRISE CONTI CHILD

BY
TARA PAMMI

MILLS
BOON

First Published in Great Britain 2016
By Mills & Boon, an imprint of HarperCollins*Publishers*
1 London Bridge Street, London, SE1 9GF

© 2016 Tara Pammi

ISBN: 978-0-263-06466-7

Tara Pammi can't remember a moment when she wasn't lost in a book—especially a romance, which was much more exciting than a mathematics textbook. Years later, Tara's wild imagination and love for the written word revealed what she really wanted to do. Now she pairs Alpha males who think they know everything with strong women who knock that theory *and* them off their feet!

Books by Tara Pammi

Mills & Boon Modern Romance

The Man to Be Reckoned With
A Deal with Demakis

Greek Tycoons Tamed

Claimed for His Duty
Bought for Her Innocence

Society Weddings

The Sicilian's Surprise Wife

A Dynasty of Sand and Scandal

The Last Prince of Dahaar
The True King of Dahaar

The Sensational Stanton Sisters

A Hint of Scandal
A Touch of Temptation

Visit the Author Profile page at millsandboon.co.uk for more titles.

PROLOGUE

LEANDRO CONTI.

The name floated, almost reverently, on the lips of the sweaty, gyrating crowd, bringing Alexis Sharpe to a sudden halt in the middle of the dance floor in an exclusive Milanese nightclub she'd only been allowed into because of her new friend, Valentina Conti.

Their friendship had been instantaneous when Alex, backpacking through Italy, had somehow found herself facing the attentions of an enamored but harmless Italian waiter. Tina had interfered and instantly decided that she liked Alex.

Valentina, vivacious, sophisticated and rich, was as different from Alex as Milan was from Brooklyn, but Alex hadn't been able to resist Tina's generous heart. The differences hadn't bothered her either until she had met Tina's older brother.

Leandro Conti... CEO of Conti Luxury Goods.
Gorgeous, sophisticated Italian magnate.

Brooding. Forbidding. Almost godlike in the way he surveyed the rest of them. As if he existed on a different sphere.

For a twenty-year-old from Brooklyn, and for one who blended into average and dull on a daily basis, that felt very true.

That he was at the nightclub in Milan was as rare as a UFO sighting. Suddenly, even the most raucous party girls pushed their hair back, adjusting dresses poured over hourglass figures.

They were hoping to catch his attention, Alexis realized, with a dawning sense of defeat.

Still, she chanced a glance.

The central glass dance floor suspended above water and the interplay of light created an illusion of a vast space. Yet the edgy elegance faded against the darkly stunning man.

That same hungry, fluttery feeling uncoiled in the pit of Alex's stomach.

Clad in a black dress shirt and dark blue jeans, the chiseled angles of his face tightly stark, he came to a standstill at the edge of the dance floor. That slate-gray gaze searched, and dismissed each face in turn.

How she longed to make sure he noticed that she, Alexis Sharpe, was a woman. That she couldn't be dismissed so easily...a compulsion she'd never felt before.

She faced every day that she lacked any special talent, that she'd been overlooked, even by her parents. This vacation to Milan had been a desperate escape she'd grabbed after being rejected at another high-flying Manhattan firm for a job. When she'd realized she wasn't equipped for a big career like some of her friends, that a menial job at her dad's health food store comprised her future.

A summer in Italy because you've been turned down at another job, her mom had said in that resigned tone of hers. *Rewarding failure, are we now?*

As if she hadn't expected anything different of Alex. The words had rankled but Alex needed this. A small rebellion in a life that had made her less than mediocre and thoroughly without merit.

And yet, when it came to Leandro Conti, she felt a reckless freedom, a vicious urge to stand out to him.

Like that time two weeks ago when he had arrived at

the dinner with Valentina, their brother, Luca, and their friends on the veranda overlooking the lake.

A soft breeze had rolled in from the lake and Valentina had whipped up a batch of margaritas. Alex had had just one sip and instantly put it down.

Leandro had dragged a chair out next to her, inquired over Valentina's twisted ankle, and then he'd turned that dark gray gaze on her.

"Other than chiding Tina that she is a big baby," he mimicked her tone, and Alex cursed herself for losing patience with Valentina that evening a few weeks ago, "how are you enjoying your trip, Ms. Sharpe?"

That accent of his had sent a shiver curling through her spine even as it stiffened at his condescending tone.

Shock that he'd sat down next to her had stolen speech from her. While his gaze had traversed over her messy, high ponytail, her forehead, her nose and, then briefly, her mouth.

A bare five seconds, maybe but Alex had felt the perusal like a caress.

Heat had clamped her cheeks and she gritted her teeth. "Alex, my name is Alex. Why do you refuse to say it?"

His greeting to her had always been unflinchingly polite, as if he was determined to deny her even that small satisfaction.

Valentina, both shrewd and kind, had warned Alex that her older brother wasn't someone to set her sights on.

Perversely, that warning had only intensified Alex's attraction to the man.

"Why do you shorten it to a man's name like that?" And then he had flitted that intractable gaze over the rest of her, her small breasts in her worn-out community college T-shirt, her midriff and her long legs in worn-out capris and her favorite sneakers. Moved up again. Four weeks amid Valentina and her friends dressed at the height of sophistication and it was the first time Alex wished she'd dressed up.

His thinly sculpted upper lip curled and Alex clenched tight inside. "Do you assume you are successful at hiding everything you are?" A taunt that no one else at the table could hear.

Shock buffeted her in waves as she looked inward.

Had she done that? Had she dressed to minimize herself, to willingly lay down in defeat before she could actually be rejected anyway by the world?

She met his gaze with a boldness she didn't know she had, this man who saw her so clearly. "I have no idea what you mean."

He sat at a perfectly respectable distance, yet fire uncoiled in every nerve. His warm breath feathered over the rim of her ear. "Little advice from your friend's brother, Ms. Sharpe. Stop looking at men like that." Then he looked at her again and those gray irises widened. "Unless you're fully aware of the weapon you wield."

He'd left then, without a backward glance.

Leaving Alex seething with humiliation and embarrassment and anger. Only then had she realized that he knew.

He knew that she was attracted to him.

And he had rejected her. Very thoroughly.

But she hadn't even retorted because it was as if her brain was incapable of higher functions when he was close.

Like now.

The din of the nightclub, the slow jazzy tune that had men and women around her gyrating sensuously, the sweaty crush of the crowd and the heated scent of pheromones…everything faded as she studied him.

He stood about two feet from her, and yet, she was aware of every inch of that hard, lean body, could feel herself gravitate toward him.

As if he was a black hole and she was being sucked toward him.

Hasn't he made a fool of you enough already, some tiny self-preservation instinct asked.

Alex clutched it like a lifeline, forced her legs to turn away from him.

She didn't need an arrogant Italian to ruin her hard-won holiday this summer. To make her feel as if somehow she came up short.

She already lived with that feeling every day.

This trip to Italy, this whole summer was supposed to be about escaping, about being someone other than the Alexis who failed at everything, the Alexis who was nothing but a mere shadow of everything her genius brother Adrian had been. About living before she returned to being a disappointment to her parents.

Anxious to get away, she tripped in her four-inch stilettos. A leanly muscled forearm wrapped around her waist, steadying her.

Held tightly against a hard, male chest, her breath knocked out.

"*Grazie mille*," she managed one of the two phrases she knew, breathless against the press of the corded muscles just below her breasts.

"You can barely stand in those stilettos. Just because Valentina offers a free pair of Contis doesn't mean you should wear them."

Her head jerked up, the gravelly voice tugging at her nerves.

Leandro Conti stared down that aquiline bridge of his nose. Neon blue lighting from the strobes cast blue shadows on his narrow, angular face, teasing her with flashes of his thin-lipped mouth.

The scowl on his brow straightened her spine. "Are you

implying that I'm not good enough to wear your exalted designer shoes?"

"I do not imply."

"You're a jerk, Mr. Conti."

His gaze flitted down over her neck, and her body tightly encased in a sheath dress she'd borrowed from Valentina. Even the stretchy fabric couldn't make much of her nonexistent curves.

But under his stare, Alex felt scorched, marked.

"And you...are playing hard at being a grown-up. Unsuccessfully, I might say."

"Damned if I do, and if I don't, with you. At least three men wanted to take me home tonight," she taunted recklessly, even as hurt pierced her, "so I say take your unwanted, stuffy opinion—"

His fingers tightened over her waist, but never hurting. Though his expression remained coolly remote. Alex wondered if his grip told more truth about him than his words. "Ah... I didn't realize your goal was so low.

"Did my fashion-genius brother not advise you that those sturdy jeans and neon pink sneakers suit that innocent, American girl-next-door image of yours to perfection? It is the perfect lure."

His infuriating attitude scraped. But the thing that her juvenile mind focused on was that he remembered her neon pink sneakers.

"Of all the faults I attributed to you, being a snob wasn't one."

"What did you attribute to me then?"

"Arrogance. Cynicism. As much feeling as a rock."

He let her go then, almost shoving her away from him. As if she'd hurt him.

Alex tottered again on the heels. Her ankle throbbed.

His arm shot out again, accompanied by pithy Italian

she was glad she couldn't understand. Her body felt ragged, as if someone else controlled her limbs.

"Should you be drinking when you're among strangers in a foreign country?"

The sharp, almost caustic tone of his words, *fortunately*, canceled out the sensuous web she fell into.

Oh, he made her so mad. And bold. And hot. As if every inch of her skin was on fire, hungry, desperate to be quenched with his touch.

"I had one...*one* glass of wine." But since she'd barely eaten anything all day, it had gone straight to her head. "Not that I need to explain myself to you. Back off."

One eyebrow rose in that imperious face. Arrogance dripped from the man even when he didn't understand her. "Back off?"

His palm was a heated brand on her lower back while he was a fortress of wiry strength in front. Men she'd met at college were boys compared to Leandro Conti. Ergo, her utter lack of sophistication in handling him. "Leave me alone. You're not my keeper, something in that vein."

"So do you have a keeper, back home? I don't think they're doing a good job of looking after you."

"What is this? The sixteenth century?" she quipped.

He wasn't particularly amused but there was a gleam in those gray depths. An infinitesimal softening of that mouth. "You're not quite the lost little waif I thought, are you?"

She forced a laugh to cover up the tingling she felt all over. He smelled so good, like the most decadent dark chocolate with a bitter edge to it. The one that clung to the senses long after it was consumed. The one you glutted on knowing it was going to settle into your thighs and hips. "Is it impossible for you to speak without being insulting?"

"You will not get sweet words from me, Ms. Sharpe. Barely eighteen and roaming a foreign country, staying with strangers. You might as well hang a Take Me sign around your neck. I'd never let Valentina—"

The barb landing sharp, Alex spoke through gritted teeth. "I'm twenty and I'm not Valentina."

She'd die before she admitted that, since that first night that Valentina had brought her to the Conti Villa, all she had thought of was him. That it was his dismissive look that'd had her borrowing Valentina's dress.

That it was his attention, his gaze that she had sought from day one. That the thought of leaving, of going back to her dull existence without knowing his kiss, his touch, haunted her.

"And Valentina and Luca are my friends, even if—"

"If you consider my brother a friend, if you mistake his intent toward you," he said, as his nostrils flared, and she wondered if he was disgusted or angry or both, "you're more foolish than I assumed. I should have never let Valentina bring you to the villa."

"You find my presence so objectionable that you're avoiding the villa, aren't you?"

She hadn't meant to betray that she'd noticed his absence. But he didn't deny her claim either.

Hurt was a thorn nestled deep into her skin.

"Luca and I...we understand each other perfectly," she added defiantly.

Although he was right.

A day after she had arrived at their villa, Luca had cornered her twice, teased her, kissed her. Made it clear within an hour that he'd love to make it more. Alex had a feeling Luca would take any woman to bury whatever lingered under that easy charm. And just as easily discard her the next morning.

But she hadn't been tempted, *at all*. Alex felt nothing even as she admitted that Luca was sex on legs.

The man in front of her however...he made her feel

naked and languid and achy all over, with just one look
from those gray depths. For all his grating politeness, he
made her feel as if he saw her, the Alexis that wanted to
pack a lifetime of adventure into one short summer.

Why, she'd no idea.

"Have you already slept with him then?"

If she'd been a violent person, if the amused glint in his
eyes hadn't lulled her, Alex would've slapped him then.
Instead, she slowly but firmly pushed his hand away and
threw him a disgusted look. "Is this your job then? Follow around the women Luca tangles with and silence them
with a dirty payoff—"

"I didn't intend to offend you," he offered roughly, and
Alexis almost believed that he hadn't meant to. That it was
curiosity rather than judgment in his tone.

She had it bad, if she was justifying his cheap remarks…

"Could there be a different intention?"

"You don't know Luca like I do. And you are…"

"I'm what, Mr. Conti? *The stereotypical American slut*?
Easy? Weak enough for you to insult without knowing the
first thing about me?"

Something almost like regret pinched his mouth. When
his gaze flipped open again, a storm danced within it. As
if some small part of him was uncoiling and awake. "Luca
is a…*sucker*, as you call it, for your type."

She raised an eyebrow then. Maybe not so imperious
like him but she was proud of herself. "And what type is
that?"

He sighed. Satisfaction pounded in Alex's blood, the
little sound of his capitulation a roaring defeat.

"You want your pound of flesh?"

"From the moment I arrived, you've looked at me like
I was dirt beneath your handmade Italian shoes. I want
every drop of blood that you owe me."

A hint of a smile caressed his lips, tilting one corner of his mouth up. The impact of it was like molten honey through her veins, turning her languorous and sluggish. "You're young and vivacious, a striking contrast of strength when compared to someone like Valentina. But your eyes, they betray your innocence and your vulnerability. You possess a distinct lack of artifice that is dangerously attractive. For a man like Luca with such jaded taste, you're like a fresh drink of water that might just sate his unquenchable thirst. It's enough to rouse a man's instincts, enough to make him assume, foolishly, that you need to be protected."

Heartbeat skittering all over the place, Alex stared, stunned. She had thought herself beneath his notice, inadequate to even catch his attention. "Why foolish?" she croaked.

"Because, as I'm realizing slowly, you might look innocent and vulnerable, but you're not weak."

"If that's an apology," she countered weakly, battling the fluttering feeling in her chest, "then it's the most convoluted one I've ever heard."

A couple of women, one dressed in black leather and the other a white cocktail dress, both so tight as if they were painted over their voluptuous bodies, passed them huddling Alexis toward him.

Their hushed whispers and awed mutterings were obvious enough for Alex.

Leandro Conti didn't usually hang around nightclubs. Or parade in public, she realized, in complete contrast to Luca who seemed to go out of his way to engage the media's attention.

Nor had he found her by accident. Valentina had already left.

Which meant he had come here looking... "Why are you here tonight?" When he frowned, she elaborated. "You barely seem to tolerate the normal pursuits and company like the rest of us."

"Have you studied me so thoroughly then?"

Alex blushed. How neatly he had trapped her into admitting that she'd been obsessed with him. But she'd never met anyone like him, didn't know how to hide her fascination.

His hand stayed on her elbow, separating her from the crowd. "My grandfather is convinced you're a gold digger out to get her claws into Luca. I've been ordered to make sure you don't succeed."

Her jaw fell open. Disbelief slowly cycled to righteous fury. And here she'd thought he'd come for her. "Go to hell," she whispered and took off.

Hot tears prickled behind her eyes and she resolutely locked them away. The arrogant jerk wasn't worth a single tear.

Somehow, she managed to only delve deeper into the mazelike nightclub, the sexy, almost hip-hop-like music chasing her. One minute, she was pushing through the throng, and next, she was looking at a lushly carpeted, quiet corridor with three unmarked doors.

Cursing, Alex turned around and banged into the one man she never wanted to see again.

Why was he following her?

"I told you to go—"

His fingers on her wrist viselike, he slid a card at the door and tugged her inside. "You're making a scene."

The door closed behind them with a finality that made Alex jump. But the stinging response that rose to her mouth died.

It was a VIP suite. Eyes wide, Alex studied it, a furious flush rising up through her neck.

Floor-to-ceiling glass paneling made up the far wall of

the plush suite, giving a perfect view into the dance floor and bar on the two levels.

Two lush couches stood against the far wall, adjacent to a small refrigerator. And on the other wall was a giant plasma screen that was currently turned off.

Gut swooping, she turned. "I don't think we should be here. This area…"

"I own this club, Ms. Sharpe."

Laughter, more sarcastic than warm, gurgled out of her. A villa in Lake Como, a nightclub in Milan, and a growing luxury goods collection that celebrities were crazy about—the Contis might as well be from a different planet. "Of course you do. Have you had men watching me all this time?"

The thick swath of his eyelashes shadowed his expression. "Valentina always has protection."

"And you told them to keep an eye on the American gold digger/slut, too."

"It was for your protection."

"And who protects me from you?"

The dim, somehow still classy purple lighting in the room didn't quite hide his flinch. But she was far too furious to wonder why.

"What do you intend? To lock me up here? To have me neatly packed away in one of your jets and have me dumped on the other side of Atlantic? To send me off silently into the night?" No, he wasn't allowed to dismiss her like this. Not when she felt so weak-kneed and aware of him. "You know your brother is a fast worker. What if I already have him in my *clutches*? Maybe Luca and I've already, *thoroughly*, f—"

"*Basta!*" he muttered, before his hand descended on her mouth while the other one locked her against the wall.

The rough, almost possessive grip he had on her hip branded her. But it was his gaze that held her rooted.

A flash of temper? A spark of emotion? Whatever it was, it lit his usually droll gaze.

He wasn't impervious to her.

Hot, reckless energy pounded through her, making her thrum with excitement. "You can think it, but I can't say it, Leandro?" She drawled her words, adding a lazy taunt. "At least, with Luca, I know I'll have a good time without insults."

Gray irises widened, bleeding into the dark black around.

The quiet room shrank around the two of them, an explosive current springing into life. The masculine scent of him was a whiplash against her senses, his fingertips pressing into her flesh.

Yet all Alex felt was charged up.

"Do you know what you so dangerously provoke? Are you prepared for it?"

A wealth of meaning reverberated in his statement and it lay between them, a grenade ticking away.

Drunk on the challenge in his molten gaze, Alex couldn't back down. "I don't care how wealthy you—"

His tapered fingers squeezed her palm gently. "I don't agree with my grandfather, *bella*."

"No?"

"*No.*"

"Then why did you come tonight?"

Tension filled the infinitesimal silence before he answered, "Luca told me he picked up a drunk Tina and couldn't locate you. I don't like the idea of you being out at night in Milan alone."

"You could've asked anyone else to do that. Your security team…you didn't have to come yourself. You could—"

"What you're hoping for, it will never happen, Alexis."

"You called me Alexis," she said simply, letting the warmth of his body float her away.

His head cocked to the side, and he rubbed her jaw.

Shock…he was shocked that he had said her name. The fingers that had been brushing her cheek pulled away. "Come, it is time for you to leave."

It was as if he'd slammed a door in her face.

He wasn't talking just about the nightclub or Milan, but Italy. He was telling her it was time for her to leave. Panic flared through her, but beneath it was a realization that sent her heart slamming against her rib cage. All these days…

"You want me," she accused. "You made me feel like I was the only one who felt it, as if I was gauche enough to read it all wrong—"

In a near-violent movement that sent her breath bursting through her, Leandro captured her wrists. Stilling her body from leaning into him. "This is a mistake."

Yanking her hands away from his grip, Alexis pressed her body against his.

A jagged sound wrenched out from his lips, throaty and low. Moving her hands up his chest, Alex tilted her head back. Every inch of his face was frozen in some kind of torturous agony. And she didn't intend to let him win.

She buried her mouth in the opening of his dress shirt. Velvet-smooth and hot, his skin burned against her lips. "Kiss me, just once. Show me what you feel, just once."

One hand snuck into her hair. Her scalp prickled as he tugged her up. Dark need pinched his features and Alex shivered, suddenly, finally, understanding the depth of the need he hid under that infuriatingly indifferent mask.

Anticipation roped with tension set her nerves on fire.

"You do not know who you're playing with."

She jerked back. "Am I so beneath you then?"

He shook his head. But the shadows didn't leave his eyes. "You're too young."

"I'm old enough to know what I want."

Flicking her tongue out, she tasted him. His hands vined

tight around her, flattening her nonexistent breasts against his chest, knocking the breath out of her. "You think I'll stop at one meager kiss?" Pure need punctured every word. "You think to play with my desire and walk away after a chaste embrace, to taunt me like you do these boys with your innocence?"

His warning only incensed her desire even more. "I'm not the one afraid, Leandro."

A volley of Italian fell from his mouth as she pressed her lower body to his. The ridge of his erection against her belly made her quiver.

His fingers descended on her hips, hurting her with their grip to keep her unmoving. "I will not touch my brother's seconds."

"We shared one kiss before I walked away. I'm not interested in Luca."

"You are the first woman in the world to claim that." Something flashed in his gaze even as his long fingers drew maddening circles over her wrists. "Which is why he likes you so much."

If her heart beat any faster, it would rip out of her chest. But still, she risked. And in this spine-tingling risk she took with Leandro, Alex felt more secure, more wanted than she'd ever felt in her life. "And you?"

It was as if all the walls he kept up fell down in dust and a primitive hunger filled his gaze. "I feel need, Alexis. When I look at you...all I feel is desire."

Even then, it was she that lifted her head, reached up and pressed her mouth to his. She, who had no experience with men, that wrapped her hands around his nape and refused to let go.

She that touched her mouth to his.

Soft and hot and hard at the same time, his mouth was a gateway to heaven and hell. Every nerve ending quivering, every instinct driving her forth, she ran the tip of her tongue tentatively, slowly, over that cruelly sculpted lower lip.

With a growl that made her belly tighten, finally he relented. Finally, he touched that hard, harsh mouth to hers.

Lights exploded behind Alex's eyes as if the world was a kaleidoscope of sensations and textures.

Masculine and demanding, he parted her lips and pushed in.

With his tongue and teeth, and with an expertise that made her sex shockingly wet, Leandro devoured her.

There was no playfulness, no seduction to his kiss, just as his words. It was a full-on sensual assault that left no doubt about where it was leading.

His hands skimmed everywhere—her breasts and the boldly taut nipples, her hips, the curves of her buttocks—before they crept under her dress and pulled it up.

Long fingers hitched her thigh around his hips until the heat of her was intimately pressed against the rigid length of him.

Every inch of her vibrated with excitement, desire, need, every inch of her thrummed at the sensation of power.

When he pushed her against the wall and covered her breasts with his hands, Alex whimpered.

When his fingers reached her wet core—alien and intrusive, her gaze flew to his, shocked and aroused and oh-so-willing. Her mouth dried at the stark need in those gray eyes.

Groaning, she came off the wall like a bow when he curled a finger inside her just so, driving a fork of heat through her pelvis.

When he flicked the rim of her ear with his tongue, and told her what he was going to do to her, Alex buried her mouth in his neck and gave herself over.

To the man, to the moment, to the incredible sensation of being wanted.

CHAPTER ONE

Seven years later

"Does your arm still hurt, Mamma?"

Alex tucked the quilt around Isabella and kissed her forehead. "A little, baby," she said, opting for the truth.

She was only six but Izzie somehow always knew if Alex lied to her. Or maybe it was that penetrating, deep gray gaze that Alex had never learned to handle. "But the cast should be gone in a couple more weeks and Auntie Jessie said I was healing well."

Little chubby fingers traced the yet unhealed, inch-wide scar that ran from her left temple to her eye, bisecting her brow where a shard of glass had pierced the skin. This bruise, unlike the fracture to her ribs and arm, was only skin-deep yet looked much worse.

"It scares me, Mamma," Izzie whispered in a low voice.

Tears coated Alex's throat but she resolutely swallowed them back. "But you're such a brave little girl always, baby."

Her little chin wobbled. "I am but all the days you were in hospital and me here, alone. Grandmama didn't tell me when you'd come home."

Pushing herself completely onto the little bed, Alex gathered her bundle of joy closer. "It looks scarier than it hurts. See, I'm perfectly fine, okay?"

When Izzie nodded, Alex hugged her tight. Felt the tension unwind in her little girl's body.

But fear lingered, a bitter taste at the back of her throat, leeching warmth from her very veins.

The sixteen-wheeler that had crashed into her compact sedan from the side had wrecked it into a pulp of metal. It was a miracle she'd survived, the doctor had said, and without permanent damage, too.

But all Alex could think of was the alternate scenario...

She could've lost her life.

And Izzie would be...

Like a black cloud waiting to swallow her, she felt the loss of breath, the violent impact of the air bag, of the crunch of bone and the shaft of nightmarish pain in her left arm all the way to her fingers...

The acidic taste of fear in her mouth...

Her hands shook, her skin clammy with sweat.

She buried her face in Izzie's hair and took a deep breath.

As always, the sweet smell of her little girl's skin anchored her in the now. Pushed back the nightmarish fingers of that panic to the edges...but she knew it wasn't gone for long.

Anything could trigger it, she realized, remembering the almost episode at the store that very morning when the door had banged too hard.

She couldn't go on like this, debilitated by fear.

Control, she needed control of this fear for Izzie. She needed to do something that wouldn't paralyze her like this, something that would take care of her baby whatever the future brought...

And instantly her mind went to him.

The man with blue-black hair. The man who had given Izzie her shockingly clear gray eyes and her thick, straight black hair, unlike Alex's strawberry blond curls. The man who had refused to see her again. Or speak to her. Or answer a single phone call seven years ago.

Even in that second before she'd lost consciousness, she'd thought of him. Of the desperate yet muted violence of his passion as he'd kissed her that night, of the way he'd moved inside her, of the way he had driven her to the edge of such intense pleasure that she'd thought she'd fragment into a million pieces...

One memory brought another now...

The disgusted look in his eyes after when she'd hung on to him like a limp vine, as his lust-heavy gaze slowly focused on her, followed by utter shock and disgust, of the jagged, agonized howl that had fallen from his mouth...the way he'd withdrawn immediately, righted her clothes so coldly and clinically, the way he wouldn't meet her gaze as he drove them to the hotel Valentina and she'd been staying at in Milan...

The way he'd told her that he never wanted to see her again...

But now, now that she had faced almost certain death, Alex wasn't willing to slink away in silence anymore. Even if that meant facing his rejection and failing.

Failure had haunted her throughout her entire life. She'd lived through being a disappointment, first to her parents, and then to herself, again and again, but she wouldn't be one when it came to Izzie.

She deserved security, and she, Alexis, needed the peace of mind to live her life normally again. She needed to know Izzie would be taken care of if something happened to her.

The very thought of facing Leandro Conti again made her skin prickle alarmingly. But she'd do anything for her daughter.

"One of you will marry the Rossi girl."

Impossibile!

Leandro Conti's answer reverberated inside him to his

grandfather's ultimatum but walking deeper into the study, he stayed silent.

"Sophia Rossi?" his brother, Luca asked, shock etched into his face.

"*Sì.*"

Leandro studied with interest the frail form of his grandfather, Antonio, behind the gleaming dark mahogany desk, still determined to intimidate his grandsons, while, next to him, leaning casually against the bookshelf, Luca adopted his usual devil-may-care attitude that infuriated Antonio so well.

Leandro sent his brother a warning glance. Antonio had not recovered completely from his heart attack a month ago.

Luca and his grandfather would have killed each other a long time ago, if it wasn't for him. And he was tiring of playing the referee among his family members.

He had begun when he was fourteen and at thirty-five, he was still doing it.

"We're too old for you to be arranging alliances for us, Nonno," Leandro finally said into the cutting silence. "I will not marry again. And—"

"Ordering me to," Luca interjected, "marry any woman is cursing the poor woman. Even one with steel balls like Sophia Rossi."

Something glinted in Antonio's eyes. "The only choice is which one of you will do it."

"Or what, Nonno?" Luca spat the words. "You will cut Leandro and me out of this...*venerable Conti empire*?"

Luca's tone made it clear it was anything but.

Because Luca's creative genius and Leandro's cutting-edge business practices over the past decade was what made Conti Luxury Goods a coveted designer label in Italy, and worldwide over the past three years.

That Antonio threatened them like this…it didn't bode well.

"I will inform," Antonio continued, "your sister that she's not a Conti, that she…is the product of your mother's shameful affair with her driver. I will disown Valentina publicly."

A filthy curse erupted from Luca's mouth, a fitting one while ice-cold fury filled Leandro's veins.

He had learned all through his life that Antonio would do anything for their family's business and knowing the kind of reckless, irresponsible, brutally selfish man his father had been, Leandro had even understood it.

But this was low, for a man Leandro respected, even liked sometimes.

Neither he nor Luca would let anything touch Valentina.

He swallowed the fury rising through him, and adopted an almost amenable expression. "Your heart attack has made you irascible, Nonno."

"You cannot persuade me away from my course, Leandro. I let you bring Valentina here…*your mother's shame*," he spat the words, "I even accepted her as my own, but do not think—"

"You love Valentina, I'm sure," Luca roared. "I thought you a better man than our father."

Antonio flinched. Apparently, even he couldn't stomach being compared to his son Enzo. "I accepted Valentina because that was Leandro's price to let me mold him for the Conti empire."

Luca turned to Leandro, disbelief in his eyes. "This is why you always let him rule your life?"

Leandro shrugged. "It was not a sacrifice, Luca. Snatching away the helm of the company from our father's hands, ousting him from the board of directors, marrying Rosa, they were all things I did because I wanted to. That I could protect Valentina's innocence was extra." He turned to Antonio, letting him see his anger for the first time. "Luca and I have put Conti on the global map, something even you hadn't dreamed about. What more could you want?"

"I want an heir to my dynasty." Understanding glinted in his eyes but Leandro refused it. "Enzo was an utter failure as a son, as a husband, as a father, but even he gave me heirs." Even the growl that fell from Luca's lips didn't detract Antonio. "This marriage to his daughter will silence that backstabbing Salvatore. Two birds with one rock."

Leandro shook his head. "This is not the way—"

"What choice do I have?" Antonio's voice loomed loud in the room. "You refuse to consider marriage and you..." Distaste robbed the old man of his words as he turned to Luca. "You change women like you change clothes.

"Death is not far for me, Leandro. I will not leave this world on the risk that Luca and you might be the last of the Contis."

His desk phone rang and Antonio picked it up.

Frustration raging in his veins, Leandro turned to Luca.

Both Luca and he had learned early enough in life that Antonio had a will of steel. He had built Leandro both into a weapon against his own son, their father, even as it broke his own heart. Whether he loved Valentina or not, he wouldn't back down from carrying out his threat.

"Luca—"

"Leandro, haven't you done—"

The loud click of the phone hitting its cradle punctured the silence and both of them turned to Antonio.

"It seems there is no choice."

Luca was the first to react. "What do you mean?"

"Salvatore Rossi's *daughter* has decided only one of you will do for marriage."

Thunder whooshed in Leandro's ears.

"She wants you, Leandro." His look toward Luca was

withering. "Apparently, she is smart enough to reject the Conti devil."

Luca's glittering black gaze, so much like their father's, turned to Leandro. A half smile played on his lips, and yet, Leandro had the sinking feeling that something else, something other than relief, hounded his brother. "Once again, the burden of this family falls to you, Leandro."

With that, he left the study.

In the ensuing silence, they could hear the noise from the veranda. Valentina's rapid words, along with laughter in between.

Valentina, who was all they had left of their mother...

"I begin to see the wisdom in the mode of life Luca has chosen. And the delirious freedom of hating you and this name and this...dynastic ego of yours..." With each word, his voice rose, fury pummeling him.

With shaking hands, he picked up the bottle of wine, the first that had been bottled at their Tuscan vineyard almost two decades ago, and thought of smashing it against the wall.

"Leandro..." Antonio's low entreaty only spiked his temper. Because of course, Antonio loved him. It hadn't been unconditional, true, but Antonio had been everything to the little boy who'd been shattered by his father's volatility.

But Leandro didn't throw it, didn't give in to the baser urge.

Leandro didn't believe in giving in to indulgent fits of temper, into foolish hopes that things were different, into thinking of his wants and needs before his duty or his family's well-being.

He didn't believe in being weak.

Only once in his life had he done that. Only once in his life had he lost control to the emotional turmoil that his father, and even Luca sometimes, seemed to feed on. In that moment, he had betrayed everything he stood for.

Even now, it wasn't Rosa's features he saw when he took himself in hand, when he had to appease his body's needs without seeking out dirty satisfaction in some strange woman's arms. He saw dark brown eyes, unflinchingly honest and hotly aroused, trembling pink lips, eager hands...

Shaking at the hold the memory had on him, *and his body,* Leandro put the bottle down.

"Another wife, Antonio? You have turned me into cattle."

Antonio looked tired. "To make the Conti name respectable again at all costs, to do everything that Enzo ruined, this was your choice, Leandro."

Leandro nodded. "Tell Salvatore that I will marry Sophia as soon as he pleases."

He had been alone far too long anyway. A marriage for the sake of children—he had nothing against that.

Memories of that long-ago summer crashed through Alexis as she stared at the majestic Villa de Conti, glittering against the night sky. The magnificent towering gates that they had just passed, the scent of jasmine that grew on the columns of the terrace porch, the breeze coming off Lake Como, and the glitterati of the Italian society dressed in designer wear and elegant diamonds, it was a sensory assault.

Fiercely intimidating, too.

Alex ran a hand over her white silk button-down blouse nervously, not that she could ever compete with this crowd. Dark blue jeans and white pumps finished her simple attire.

She was glad she had called Valentina. The lie had fallen so easily off her lips—that she was touring Italy again and would love to see her. Valentina had sounded delighted, pretending as if they had remained friends after that summer instead of Alex calling her out of the blue. Had even sent Alex a car to pick her up.

But she hadn't mentioned that Alex would be arriving at the villa the night of, what seemed like, a big party.

Thanking the driver, Alex exited from the car and looked up. Now that she stood there, anxiety made her empty stomach heave. Her mouth felt dry.

How was she supposed to locate *him* amid this crowd, much less tell him about Izzie?

Alex swayed, some primal instinct urging her to turn around and flee. But Izzie's welfare and her own peace of mind depended on this.

Shaking at the warring logic and instinct, she froze.

"Alex? Alexis Sharpe?"

Luca Conti stood at the top of the steps, looking dashing in a black tuxedo. The usual, ornamental blonde on his arm was such a familiar sight that Alex felt a burst of affection. She had a feeling he'd been on his way out.

While she tried to get her vocal chords to work, Luca dismissed the blonde and came down the steps.

Vitality radiated from him, an easy smile on his lips. As he came closer, the cast of those similar features left her reeling afresh.

Before she could blink, she was enfolded in a tight hug. Alex returned it slowly, her throat thick, her limbs shaking.

Why hadn't she tangled with this easy man, the desperate and shameful thought popped up.

Luca pulled back, studied her at leisure with those deceptively mocking black eyes. His grip around her waist tightened, in comfort, she realized as her shaking refused to cease.

"You've become stunning, *bella*. I knew I shouldn't have let you go that summer."

Alex smiled, grateful for his tease. "Thank you, Luca. Valentina knew I was coming. I…"

"But, of course, you are welcome, Alex." She could see the curiosity in his eyes, but he didn't press. Instead he offered her his arm. "Come, let us find something for you to drink and then we find Valentina, *si*?"

Alex shook her head. She had almost lost her nerve earlier, but not anymore. "I will see Valentina later, maybe. Luca…will you take me…can you please arrange for me to see your brother?"

"Leandro…" Shock reflected in his gaze as it met hers. "You came to see Leandro." It was not a question.

"Yes."

"It is not anything I could help with, *bella*?" he sounded sympathetic.

"No."

Something flickered in his gaze before he looked up at the villa, and then back at her but this time, his look was different, the playfulness gone. Alex was sure he'd deny her.

"Then let us go find my esteemed brother." Relief made her shiver. "I have to warn you, though, *cara*, that he is quite in demand, especially tonight. It will take us some time to reach him. Have patience, *si*?"

"Yes."

Her legs barely holding her up, Alex half leaned on Luca's arm. Her thudding pulse was a violent cacophony in her ears as they walked into the marble floored foyer and searched for that tall, lean frame that had haunted her dreams for seven years.

Alexis…

He'd thought he'd seen her an hour ago, her face paler than the simple, white silk blouse that clung to her curves.

Leandro had never been quite so shocked in his entire

life as he'd been the moment he spied that lithe figure on Luca's arm.

For a few minutes, he had stood there, stock-still, wondering if he was hallucinating. Wondering if the eve of his engagement to Sophia had unlocked the one face he had tried to bury in the deepest recesses of his mind.

Wondering if his one sin was finally catching up to him.

Until Sophia had put a hand on his shoulder slightly and called his name.

He'd turned to her, offered a quick smile and then slowly, his very sanity up for question, searched that same spot again.

There had been no Luca or her.

The long evening dragged on and on until Salvatore Rossi had paraded him in front of all the guests, boasting quite shamelessly that his daughter had snared a dynastic connection like Conti.

And *Leandro Conti* of all.

Even Sophia had cringed at some point. Who, Leandro admitted, he liked.

There was something self-sufficient and intelligent and very contained about her. At least, he would have a comfortable marriage, he realized halfway through the evening, free of all the marital drama he'd seen between his own parents.

Valentina's innocence or not, he couldn't take a marriage like that.

Within minutes of meeting her, Sophia had put his mind at ease.

He'd danced with her as the band played a slow jazz, then with his sister, who had chatted on and on about some old friend.

It was past ten and Leandro found himself in the private sitting lounge on the first floor, away from the still celebrating guests.

Salvatore Rossi and Sophia, Valentina, his grandfather, two of his aunts and two of his dissolute cousins were present. Luca had acted strangely, even for him, ever since Antonio had announced this merger.

Leandro was about to go looking for him when he appeared at the entrance and behind him, walked in the one woman Leandro never ever wanted to see again in his entire life.

The woman who'd known his one moment of weakness, the loss of his control…

Valentina's cheerful greeting reverberated loud in the silence of the room, the clatter of her heels on the parquet floor as she went to the woman deafening.

It *was* Alexis he had seen earlier.

A neatly cut black jacket delineated slender shoulders. A silk blouse clung to a lush figure that he didn't quite remember like that. She had been lithe, almost gaunt, breakable in his large hands…and yet so violently passionate… as if only Leandro could give her what she needed most.

Maledizione!

He was mad to be wondering about her body and yet his gaze continued its perusal of her with a mind of its own.

Dark blue jeans hugged her long legs, legs she had wrapped around him as he…his blood drifted south slowly, a heady thrill filled his veins, a feeling he had never known except that night…

Leandro gritted his teeth, willing his body under his command. One look at her and he was ready to react like an uncouth youth.

He lifted his gaze to her face, and stared in shock.

A jagged scar began somewhere beneath her hairline and went through her left brow, the skin puckered. Yet didn't minimize her appeal. If anything, it added even more character to the strong lines of her face.

She was no dazzling beauty, then or now.

Hers was more insidious, seeping under one's skin before you realized, the kind that enthralled the more you looked.

It lay in that high forehead, the intelligence that shone in those tilted, light brown eyes, the irresistible combination of innocence and confidence in the way she greeted the world, the too-bold nose and the lush, wide, implausibly gorgeous mouth. In how sinuously she trapped one's attention, drawing in like a spider with her silky web.

She had been a roughly stunning sketch in black-and-white then. Now, now she was a hauntingly beautiful painting that had grown into its promise, that would bestow pleasure for years to come.

Her brown eyes, bold and direct, searched the room and settled on him.

A pure bolt of energy flew between them, locking them together as if they were the only people in the room, in the world.

Something inside him, something only she had known leaped and growled at the sight of her again.

Her skin paled under the brilliance of the crystal chandelier even as she held his gaze stubbornly. She held her left hand awkwardly against her body.

Cutting his gaze away from her, which took far too much effort, Leandro stifled the life out of that strange fever in his veins.

Why was she here now, after seven years? On the eve of my engagement of all nights?

Before he could voice a question, Antonio's stringent words shattered the choking quiet. "It is family here tonight, Luca. Your dirty playthings are not welcome."

Alexis flinched. When Luca would have interrupted, she stilled him with a hand on his arm. His usually volatile brother relented with a shrug.

Something ugly erupted in Leandro's gut. *Dio, she would make me jealous of his own brother?*

Leandro saw her falter, pull a deep breath and then face Antonio. "I'm not Luca's...*plaything*, Mr. Conti, nor *will I leave* before I say what I intend." Then she leveled that resolute gaze at him. "I need to speak to you alone."

Leandro hardened himself against the beseeching look in her eyes. After seven years, that she showed up tonight of all nights, there was only one thing she could be after— money. And that *perversely* made him angrier. "There is nothing you could say to me that you could not say here, Ms. Sharpe."

"Leandro..." his brother again.

Leandro held up his hand, more than furious now.

How long had Luca been in touch with her? How could there be such...a friendship between them if not so?

And why the hell did he care whatever was between them?

He skewered the woman with his gaze. "Whatever game you're up to, I'm not playing."

Anger burned in her eyes, her lithe body faintly trembled with it. "Fine, so be it." Her voice rang crystal clear in the rapt room, and still he could hear the tremble in it. "I came to tell you that you... *I* have a daughter." Her chin rose. "Her name is Isabella Adrian. She's six years old and she's beautiful and precious and she...*she's yours*."

"No," fell from Leandro's lips, a snarling whisper in the quiet room. "That can't be."

His grandfather's and Salvatore Rossi's curses in Italian and Valentina's muffled gasp registered on the periphery of his consciousness.

Lips quivering, Alexis's chest rose and fell but she held his gaze over the distance. "A DNA test will prove I'm right," she said, as if she'd prepared the response. But it was the absolute purpose in her voice that held him mute.

A daughter...

His skin felt chilly as if all warmth had been leeched away from the world around him.

And yet, the crystal chandeliers in the room glowed bright, the fire cackled in the marble-wrought fireplace and the moon hung jewel bright in the sky outside.

The world continued spinning whereas all of the control he prided himself on deserted him, leaving him shaken to the core.

He shook his head, gasping for breath.

He looked at Luca. Who looked just as aghast as he did.

Only Alexis stood composed amid the curious and accusing glares aimed at her, her shoulders ramrod straight.

Alexis whose eyes gleamed with pride and love as she claimed that he was a father. Of her little girl.

His child...something Rosa had wanted so desperately for years.

Now, this woman, whom he'd tried to forget, claimed her daughter was his...*that his one moment of weakness had led to such a consequence?*

Everything inside him clenched tight, as if the merest breath could shatter him. Robbing him of speech even.

"Whatever your scheme, Ms. Sharpe, you have already made a misstep in your bait." Antonio finally spoke, his accented English falling like hard gravel over the marble floor. "If there were Conti bastards lying around for you to sully our name with, your claim would be believable if you said Luca fathered them.

"Not Leandro.

"Now before I call the *polizia—*"

CHAPTER TWO

"Enough!" ALEX BIT OUT, her throat raw. Leandro's silence distressed her more than his grandfather's words. "I won't stand quietly while you call my little girl names."

She felt Luca's hand on her shoulder and drew strength from it.

Faking defiance she didn't feel, Alex held Leandro's gaze.

Disbelief? Disgust? Something finally flickered in his expression and she felt as if she was bucking, bending against the force of it.

Aquiline nose, thinly sculpted mouth and the sleek, sharp planes of his face...he was just as arrogantly beautiful as she remembered.

Seven years hadn't changed his feelings about that night then. She hadn't hoped differently, neither would she let him shame her.

She had done nothing to be shameful of. *Not then, not now.*

"You stay silent even as you know there's a chance that it's true? I was wrong to come here, wrong to think Izzie..." She took a bracing breath. "You and your family, you don't deserve to know her."

Alexis turned her back on them with her head held high.

Out into the corridor she went, her pumps clicking hard on the gleaming marble floor, ignoring the hollow ache in her gut.

It was the uncertainty caused by the accident, the uncertainty about Isabella's future, she told herself. Nothing to do with the man who stood there, unmoving like a rock while his family castigated her.

Having arrived at the end of the corridor, Alex stilled.

Approaching dusk hadn't dimmed the beauty of the villa one bit.

The corridor opened into a semicircular balcony, offering a view to the ground floor, the acreage surrounding the house lit up by solar lights and the dark waters of the lake beyond.

A tinkle of laughter from the guests below her brought her attention back. Pressing a hand to her throbbing temples, she faced her current problem.

She couldn't ask Valentina for a ride back. Would Luca help?

She turned and slammed headlong into a solidly male body. Threaded her fingers in that hard chest for purchase. "Luca, can you please…"

Crisply masculine and with a hint of aqua, the scent that filled her nostrils arrested the words on her lips. Her head jerked up so fast that she felt dizzy.

Penetrating gray eyes studied her.

"Why assume Luca?"

"Because he seems like the only decent person in your family."

She tugged at her arm but Leandro didn't relent. Her legs tangled with his, the hard, muscular length of his thighs against hers knocking the breath out of her.

Hard and hot, he made her head spin. "I have nothing more to say to you," she breathed into his shoulder.

"You think to announce what you did and walk away calmly? Probably into the media's mouthpiece? Make a mockery of the Contis?"

His grip viselike, he dragged her through a turn in the corridor that led to another sit-out area and then past a dark oak door. The hard thud of the door cut off the noise from the party, locking them away.

Breath rattling, Alex kept her back to him.

Her skin prickled at his nearness, her senses still jarred at the impact with his hard body. She rubbed fingers over her forehead, willing her heart to calm.

Slowly, she took in the sumptuous furnishings in the huge room, a dark mahogany study table to the side with papers strewn on it, the large four-poster king bed with dark blue sheets. That same cool aqua scent clung to the room. A small, framed picture sat on the nightstand on the opposite side, of a pretty woman with dark hair and delicate features.

Dear Lord, was this his room? Who was that woman then?

With her gut in a tight knot, Alex forced her gaze to the window. The view afforded here of Lake Como was even better. Spectacularly maintained gardens, acres of it, lit softly by moonlight and solar lights along the paths greeted her. Silence lingered in this part of the gardens.

Even his guests were not allowed to impinge on his private slice of heaven, she realized slowly.

This estate was not just beautiful but huge.

And this was only one of the many properties they owned.

The Contis were a dynastic family with an old-world wealth and Leandro…at the helm of it. And she had barged in on their illustrious party and told them that he had a daughter.

If her chest wasn't so tight, Alex would have laughed at the absurdity of it.

"You're afraid to face me now? After that performance in front of everyone."

Low and crisp, his tone was like fingertips sliding over

her bare skin. As if it was yesterday he had touched her and not seven long years ago.

Alex turned slowly, loathe to betray how unbalanced she felt in his presence.

He stood leaning against the closed door, minus the suit jacket, the gray of his dress shirt making his eyes gleam doubly. Leaner than she remembered, his features sharper. Even more settled into that powerful aura that had always clung to him.

The austere severity of his features from the sculpted jaw to that aquiline nose, the lean, wiry breadth of his chest tapering to a waist, the thinly sculpted curve of his lower lip, everything about Leandro Conti said leashed power.

Any moment now, she wouldn't find him attractive. Any moment now, she'd remember that the same mouth that could kiss so passionately and tenderly could also shred her to pieces as soon as he was done.

"I'm trying to overcome my shock that you cared enough to stop me." Instead, her insides thrummed with a thrill. "And if that was a performance, then you forced me to it."

Those eyes of his studied her relentlessly. Why didn't the infuriating man say anything? Demand a DNA test? Throw her out if he didn't believe her? Threaten her like his grandfather had done?

She had been prepared for all of that. Except his impenetrable silence, this unnerving composure.

It made her want to take a sledgehammer and smash it to pieces.

"You pulling me into a room like this, away from prying eyes should bring back memories for you," she threw recklessly. "Lucky for me, because it seems you erased that evening from your mind."

His chin jerked, and his eyes lost that inscrutable expression. "I was successful. Until this very evening."

Alex blinked at the hurt that pinged through her, as if her poisonous dart had found its way back to her. She didn't think he was saying it to get a rise out of her, like she'd done.

No, he merely stated fact.

"What would you have dared to remind me, Alexis?"

Her name on his lips was a possessive caress that threatened her paper-thin composure.

Suppressing the dangerous urge to take up the challenge in his tone, she said, "Your assumption that I'm dying to… *renew* our acquaintance smacks of arrogance. I'm here only for Isabella."

Whether he believed her or not, Alex didn't know. But then, from what little she knew of Leandro, he thrived on self-control. That he hadn't instantly called her a liar like his grandfather had done, his utter silence in the face of her declaration, said something else entirely, she realized with a little panic.

He circled the room, moving a thing here and there and finally, leaned against the bed. "How are you here, today?"

"I don't understand."

"How did you come to be here at the villa, tonight of all nights? Did you know—?"

"About the party? Of course not. You think I wanted to make a spectacle of myself in front of your exalted family? Valentina must have decided tonight was best."

One haughty brow rose on his face. "For what?"

"I hinted, pretty heavily, that I wanted to say hello to you and Luca. She assumed that I was eager to renew my friendship with Luca."

"And Luca?" The two words rang with his displeasure.

Frustration made her voice sharp. "What about Luca?"

Something flashed in his gaze, the first sign that maybe he wasn't so composed. "How did you arrive on his arm?"

Of all the things he had said and unsaid today, this annoyed her most. "He was kind enough to escort me to you when I insisted on seeing you."

"You told me that night that you were protected."

The sudden shift in the conversation caught her off guard. "I was. I began the pill a few weeks before I left for Italy."

"In preparation for your fling abroad?"

His barb pricked her, but she'd rather he believe that he'd been the convenient choice. The one man she'd picked out of a lineup to have her supposed holiday fling with. "I was in over my head from the minute I saw you, yes." Resentment she'd swallowed for years flared. "What's your excuse then?"

"You think I blame you for that night." The idea seemed to shock him.

What else was she supposed to think, she wanted to throw back at him. Even now, he looked at her as if she was his worst nightmare. There was no point in scraping old wounds however. "Even the pill is not one-hundred-percent foolproof." He remained silent again and it began to scrape Alex raw. "If you don't believe me, then—"

"Since I'm still feeling the consequences of that...*very activity* seven years ago, I believe I will refrain from it."

"That's not an invitation. This trip isn't a ploy to renew that...madness. You probably find this hard to believe but not every woman wants a piece of your esteemed Conti pie." She was so angry she wanted to thump the man.

"Really?"

He made it so easy to despise him with his insufferable attitude.

To pretend that her skin hadn't prickled, her heart hadn't raced, that even the thought of Izzie had disappeared in that moment when she had spied him again in that lounge. To act as though, for seven years, she hadn't relived every moment with him a thousand times.

"Yes. I have too much self-respect to be attracted to a man who thinks I'm a liar and worse. To want a man who dismissed me like garbage back in my life."

Faint lines appeared around his mouth before he looked away.

Bloodthirsty enough after that scene in the lounge, Alex felt feral satisfaction that she'd landed another one.

"Why did you wait seven years to…make this claim?"

"Calling it a claim will not make it less of a truth." The taunt was instant and yet…she had a feeling it had taken him this long to work toward the subject of Isabella, to acknowledge the ticking bomb between them.

He pushed off the bed and Alex needed all her will power to not step back. "Did you think I would have no questions for you at all?" She remained silent and he continued. "Why didn't you let me know immediately?"

"By the time I realized I was…pregnant, I was almost ten weeks along."

"Is that why you kept…the baby?" He raised a hand to cut her off. "You were twenty. I…cannot imagine Valentina mature enough to manage herself, much less a child at that age."

Alex swallowed, the utter strength of her conviction that day amazing her even now. Her parents, her only close friend, everyone had advised her to give up the baby for adoption. "I just…" She shied her gaze away, her throat thick with emotion.

"Tell me why."

Jerked by his sharp tone, she lifted her gaze. "That feeling…it's inexplicable."

Something so raw and visceral flashed in his gaze that her skin prickled. Arrogant, heartless, cynical…she'd made her decision to come here based on the fact that Leandro was all those things. What if she was wrong?

Fear pulsed down her spine. "I called your office a week

after I found out. I... I was on hold for an hour. Finally, when your secretary came on, she cut me off, said you weren't interested.

"That I shouldn't call back." Alex tried to keep any complaint out of her voice now however anxious she'd been then. "I called you a few more times. Got the same answer again."

"You could have called your friend, Luca." He spoke softly, yet it cracked through the room like a gale of wind. "You could have come back to Italy. You could have told Valentina. You could have emailed me—"

"And what? Capitalized the subject line—*I'M PREG-NANT, IT'S YOURS*—like some spammer!" She colored furiously. "You wanted nothing to do with me. But... I still tried.

"I bought another ticket. I...thought you should know. The day before I was supposed to leave, my parents and I argued and my dad threw out his back at the store. I... I couldn't go off in search of you then, especially when you were determined to forget me.

"With taking care of the store and him, when Isabella came... I barely had the energy to go through each day."

"And later?"

How dare he sound as if it was her fault? "Later," she said, feeling suddenly tired, "it was easier to believe that Izzie was better off without your rejection." Easier to protect herself from the hurt he had wreaked on her.

The one time she had taken a chance to reach for something she'd wanted, she'd been rejected. Firmly pushed back into the forgettable category again.

There had been nothing special or memorable about her or that night for him. As if she was a mere blip in the life of another person yet again.

A disappointment, an inconvenience, a thing with no value or feelings whatsoever.

"Why did you change your mind now?" he bit out harshly. He ran his fingers through his hair while he paced the small room like a caged animal. "Or was that your plan all along?"

"Wouldn't that be perfect for you if I had some ultimate agenda? If I proved your worst assumptions about me right? That way you won't have to take any responsibility in all this…"

"*Dio,* why now, Alexis?"

It was his hoarse voice that halted Alex's self-indulgent tirade. This was not about her feelings. This was about her baby.

"I just… I was in an accident three months ago, a bad one." Automatically, her fingers went to the scar down her forehead and his gaze moved there. Throat raw, she continued, "It made me realize…if something happened to me, Isabella would be alone in the world. My parents…" She swallowed the fact that they had never approved of her having Isabella. "They're growing old. I can't sleep wondering about her future."

Once again, silence descended, his stare unnerving her on a whole new level.

"I brought her birth certificate," she said, busying herself with the handbag. "Just tell me where and when to bring her for the DNA test, although it'll be a huge help if it's in New York because I can't—"

"There's no situation that fazes you, is there? You set your course and you blaze through it, come what may."

Alex blanched. Softly delivered but his innuendo pierced just the same.

He thought this was easy for her? To see him after all these years, to realize that he still viewed her with that loathing? To know that she'd never been anything more than a quick indulgence?

But she swallowed her own feelings and focused on

what she needed to do. "I'm prepared to do anything to prove that she's yours, yes."

"And, in return?"

"Are you so afraid of what I would demand, Leandro?" The challenge escaped her before she could catch it, her femininity rearing its head.

An almost imperceptible widening of those stormy eyes. Something she wouldn't have even noticed if she wasn't so greedy about every nuance on his face.

"Do you have many to make then, Alexis? These demands?"

Why was she taunting him? Why this reckless, dangerous urge to provoke him? She pulled out the envelope she'd stuffed into her handbag. "Here's some pictures. Maybe you could visit us and meet Izzie a couple of times over the next couple of years so that you aren't a complete stranger? I could bring her here for holiday, to meet Luca and Valentina, if they're interested.

"All I want is a promise that if anything were to happen to me, you'd…"

Her words trailed away as Leandro became still. The muscles in his face pulled taut over his features, a white pallor to his olive skin.

Her outstretched hand lay between them. And his gaze on the envelope, frozen.

"Leandro?"

The swath of his eyelashes flickered. His rough breath rattled loud in the room.

With gut-wrenching clarity, Alex realized that he'd rather she was lying.

From the moment she'd spoken Isabella's name, it wasn't the veracity of her claim he'd doubted. What had kept him silent, even as his grandfather had shredded her, was that Leandro *needed* her to be lying.

"You wish Isabella didn't exist." Horror filled her, turning her voice into a whiplash. "Do you despise me that much?"

He jerked around, pain streaking through his eyes. "What I feel about her has nothing to do with you."

That's good, she told herself. She couldn't bear it if he despised Isabella like he did her. She wouldn't allow it.

How much do you know of that man? Her mom's question came back to her now.

She didn't know that much, really.

Her intense attraction to him seven years ago, her fascination with him, the connection she'd felt with him, had been inexplicable. She stole another greedy glance at him, unable to stop herself. Lean and tall, he wore his power effortlessly and she wondered if that had been the draw for her.

Hands shaking, she stuffed the envelope back into her handbag. She needed to leave. Before she made this about her. Before she asked any more of those stupid questions…

Before she forgot that this man had crushed her tender heart in such a way that it hadn't mended again.

"Show me the pictures," Leandro finally forced himself to say.

Alexis stilled with her back to him, her slender shoulders a tense line.

His voice sounded as if he hadn't used it in years, as if forming such simple words was beyond his capability. Told himself again and again that he was composed.

If he acted like it, he hoped his rioting emotions would catch on that he was composed, that he would survive through this new development in his life like he always did.

Giving in to the shame that he had behaved in a way he detested was only self-indulgent. Giving in to the guilt that clawed at him that he had abandoned his child…would only render him useless.

His head jerked up, the realization that he believed Alexis stunning him anew.

He believed that she was telling the truth, that her daughter was his?

Antonio would call him a fool, their lawyers would tell him to demand a DNA test. The rational, sensible part of him, which had been born out of necessity at a young age, warned that he was being reckless. That Alexis's poise, her self-sufficiency, her declaration that she wanted nothing from him, that they all could be lies.

She could have waited all these years just so she could make a bigger splash, demand a bigger payoff.

He wasn't unaware of his draw for women. If they fell like flies for Luca's charm, they went rabid because of how sacrosanct his privacy was to him, because the media, frequently and fervently, painted him as the perfect man, still mourning his wife.

Yet that same instinct that had drawn him to her drowned out everything else. "Show me the pictures."

Knuckles turning white, her fingers tightened over the straps of her bag. Her reluctance now would have been comical, if not for the fierce churning in his gut. "I didn't come to force you to be a father."

He moved closer, uncaring of the tremble in her lips, the slight widening of her eyes. Crowded her lithe body against the door, his self-discipline in tatters now. "You are afraid now? After you came all this way?"

Something in his tone must have finally registered because she pulled out the envelope.

He moved back toward the bed and spread them out on the dark cover.

There were ten, different sizes and in different poses.

His heart thundering, he picked up one eight-by-ten, a close-up. With jet-black hair that framed her face and serious gray eyes, and the cast of her features, drawn in chubbiness instead of sharp planes, the little girl was his mirror image.

The girl, *no, Isabella*...was his daughter. His own flesh and blood.

"There is nothing of me in her," came Alexis's reply behind him. Tentative and reverberating with a quiet joy. "Every morning, I look at her and I'm amazed that she's mine."

Inhaling roughly, he turned.

Raw emotion glittered in her eyes. Walking closer, unaware of her own actions, he was sure, she studied him avidly. He knew she was seeing her daughter, *no, their daughter* in his face.

Still, her gaze was like a physical caress. Possessive and hungry and intent. And deeply disconcerting for the instant ache it evoked in him.

He looked at the picture and then at Alex. "That determined chin, that's you."

A smile curved her mouth, transforming her into a stunning beauty. "Really?"

"Where is she now?" he asked, more to distract himself from the scent of her fluttering toward him. Subtle yet lingering. Like the woman herself.

"With my parents. Isabella and I live with them. A friend of mine has a boy of Izzie's age and she takes her during the day. You can keep the pictures." She looked through her bag and extracted visiting cards and extended them to him. Like a salesgirl pushing a product. "These have all my numbers and email address. Just call me in advance, because after the accident and this trip, I can't take off more—"

"In advance for what?" he repeated.

She shrugged but hurt shadowed her eyes. "Y'know... if you decide to see her."

He emerged from the emotional knockout, her intention in all the things she had told him tonight shaping into coherence. His gut tightened.

When he made no move to take the cards, she put them on the small study table. "I'll be in Milan for two more days if you have any questions." She worried her bottom lip between her teeth. "If you can arrange a car for me, I'll be off."

A growl he couldn't control emerged low in Leandro's throat.

She thought she would show him pictures of his daughter and then bid him goodbye? That he would call her and make an appointment like some distant relative?

Did she think he had no honor, no sense of duty?

Have you treated her like you have any?

"Stay tonight," he finally said, somehow managing to keep his tone smooth. A herculean feat seeing that his head was in a whirl, his world precariously tilted on its axis. And this woman, whom he'd tried to forget at all costs, suddenly was at the center of it. "You look like you'll faint any minute."

"I don't want to cause trouble—"

"Little late for that, yes?" He slid the pictures back into the cover. "Someone from the staff will show you to a bedroom. *Buenonotte*, Alexis."

Leandro paced inside his bedroom, the scent of a woman lingering inside the walls after so many years as disconcerting as the one who had left it behind. A million thoughts crowded him.

He remembered his secretary telling him that Ms. Sharpe had called. *Again and again.* He remembered the self-disgust at the mere thought of that night, the poisonous thoughts that Alexis was making a nuisance of herself.

Because he had had enough with his father's mistresses and one-night stands making a spectacle of them.

And the intervening years, if he focused too much on that, he would take it out on her.

Despite everything, she had finally come to tell him of his daughter's existence. The *what if she hadn't* scenario didn't bear thinking about…not if he wanted to remain sane.

With control he had learned in his teens, because someone had had to be strong for his mother and Luca, he bottled away the anger.

The Rossis would be waiting for an explanation, as would Antonio. His engagement to Sophia had been the biggest event of the summer among society and Salvatore wouldn't react to this new development lightly.

Leandro would have to make sure Salvatore didn't poison anyone on the Conti board against him because of any decision he took now.

He'd have to make sure Antonio didn't interfere with Leandro's intentions.

He'd have to tread carefully so that his sheer arrogance in dismissing Alexis seven years ago didn't ripple over anyone now. Like Valentina and Sophia. *And now Isabella.*

She was his to protect, to cherish, to love. A shock or not, he could never neglect his duty as a father. A child needed both parents, he knew that better than anyone.

He vowed in that minute that the next generation of Contis would be different, beginning with Isabella. Much as he'd tried, he'd failed Luca.

He wouldn't fail Isabella. He wouldn't let his daughter spend a day without knowing that she was loved and wanted.

If Alexis had other ideas, he would convince her otherwise.

The weight of the world seemed to lie on his shoulders and yet, Leandro felt energized for the first time in years.

CHAPTER THREE

JUNE SUN SHONE bright when Alex stepped out of her room and reached the curving balcony. A vague sense of premonition hovered in her gut, intensified by her sleepless night.

Something she had spied in Leandro's eyes, she realized.

"Alex, come have breakfast," came Valentina's voice from below.

Bracing herself, Alex looked down. It was only Valentina.

She went down the steps and walked across the courtyard to the perfectly landscaped gardens. Lushly scented air filled her nostrils, the sheer beauty of the surroundings relaxing her tautly stretched nerves.

Dressed in chic jeans and a ruffled top in pink, her hair *fashionably* messy, Valentina was the epitome of a fashionista. Alex was suddenly glad she wasn't wearing yesterday's clothes.

Plain cotton T-shirts, of the soft and screamingly expensive kind, and capri-style pants in various sizes and colors, even brand-new underwear had been left on the bed by the time she had returned from the shower.

Knowing who she had to thank for it, she ran a self-conscious hand over her midriff and settled down.

A bite of the rich, jam-filled *cornetto* the staff brought her righted her world, even if for a moment. The frothy cappuccino made her sigh.

Feeling Valentina's gaze on her, she lifted hers. "If I apologize for using you, it'll be false."

Valentina nodded, a thoughtful look in her eyes. "I did not see Leandro again last night. Luca says he believes you."

Comforted by Luca's easy acceptance, Alex clicked her cell on.

Valentina looked at Izzie's pic and let out a soft sigh. "I'm sorry for what my grandfather said," she offered, and Alex waved her away. The apology she wanted wasn't Valentina's. Not even Antonio's, as insulting as he'd been.

"Alex, you cannot...*imagine* how shocking this is for us—"

"I do—"

"*No!* That Leandro...was with you, and so soon after... That's not like him."

"What, he doesn't have sex like normal people?" Alex retorted, her skin prickling.

Valentina made a face. "Gross...but *si.* You know what the media calls Leandro and Luca?"

"What?"

"The Conti Saint and the Conti Devil."

"Callously dismissing the woman you just slept with makes for a saint in your country?"

"You do not understand—"

"I don't need to," Alex cut her off bluntly and the curiosity within.

She didn't want to know about Leandro's love life. Or why he had behaved so ruthlessly with her. Or that he was, apparently, the embodiment of the perfect man to the rest of the freaking world.

"Your timing...sucks," Valentina sounded sympathetic. "Seven years ago and last night."

How are you here, tonight of all nights...?

"Wait, what was last night?"

"Leandro's engagement party."

Engagement...it landed like an invisible punch, jostling

her insides. He could have married in the past seven years, could've had a string of lovers like her...

Thoughts tripped one over the other.

Was it that woman standing next to him? The woman on whose shoulder his hand had rested? Did he treat her better than he had Alex? Was it because Alex lacked...

No!

Nothing ever came out of berating herself that she wasn't good enough or memorable enough to hold the attention of a man like Leandro Conti.

Why would a stranger she'd built a fantasy around see anything special in her when her own parents didn't?

A besotted, naive novelty, that's what she'd been.

"It doesn't matter if he's engaged or has a string of play-things and mistresses spread out over the Italian coast, Valentina," her words came out harsh. "I don't care about Leandro."

"That heartens me," a crisply smooth voice interfered from behind her, "so much. It's almost *saintly* how unin-terested you're in the life of the man you share a daugh-ter with."

Sarcasm dripped from Leandro's every word. Sweet pastry instantly turned to ash in Alex's mouth. "Maybe it's time someone told you that you're not the great prize every woman falls over for."

"You assume this is what I think of myself? Why?"

"Your sheer disbelief that I'm not throwing myself at you, again," she snapped back.

With a wide-eyed grin, Valentina neatly slipped away.

Clasping her quivering fingers in her lap, Alex looked up. The sun directly behind him delineated the broad shoulders and the tapering waist while the breeze drenched her in his crisp, masculine scent.

The dark jeans and black shirt molded his lean frame.

The impact of such sheer masculinity was nerve-racking after another sleepless night.

Seven years hadn't dimmed his appeal even a bit. If anything...

Don't go there, Alex!

"Congratulations on your engagement." Steady and serene, she almost believed it herself.

He took her offered hand after a moment and clasped it.

Rough and abrasive and large, his palm stroked a dart of heat through her.

Alex jerked it back, like a frightened rabbit, heart pumping hard.

"*Grazie*, Alexis." Mockery laced with politeness. "Hope you'll forgive me if I don't introduce my fiancée to you. It might prove a little tacky after the shock she received on the eve of her engagement."

Her cup rattled on the saucer loudly in the peaceful courtyard, his sickly sweet tone jarring her. "I didn't know or I would've never—"

"I know."

His instant accord took the sails away from under her. "Neither did I come here hoping for some fat payoff."

"So you will refuse if I set up a trust fund for Isabella then?"

She quickly swallowed her shock. And the oily, uncomfortable feeling in her throat. "No. I...manage okay but I won't refuse something that'll surely help Izzie's future." It galled her to admit defeat in so many words, to recount her failure to a man who made everything he touched into gold. But for Izzie, she had to. "The accident, on top of some bad business decisions I made last year... everything's been tight. College tuition when she's ready is going to be astronomical."

His protracted look stung as she realized how he must view her ready answer. Defensive on top of feeling like a failure made her spine rigid and her tone caustic. "I have a six-year-old, a health store that's afloat for now and aging parents. I'm practical, not a piranha."

"Did I imply otherwise?"

"Whatever you decide, you can lock it up. I won't touch it."

Their gazes held, his inscrutable and hers confused.

If he believed that she hadn't known about his engagement, *and* that she wasn't looking for a retirement package in the name of Izzie, then why was there was a storm of fury beneath his smooth tone?

Why such a distant, adversarial glint in his eyes when he looked at her?

But asking meant getting personal. Asking meant allowing herself to examine why the news of his engagement sat like a jagged boulder on her chest. Asking meant learning how little of an impression she had left that night.

For as long as she could remember, her mom and her own failures at everything remotely related to academia and a career had made Alex clearly aware of all her shortcomings. She'd been measured, again and again, first against Adrian and then against his ghost and had come up short every time.

She didn't want to hear it from the man who had been an escape and a gift she'd given herself, too.

"I should be leaving," she said into the silence.

He flicked her a quick glance and nodded. "We'll leave in ten minutes."

Alex whirled toward him so fast that she lost her balance. A corded forearm pressed into her belly holding her up.

She closed her eyes, the heat of him stroking every suppressed desire.

Heart rapping a staccato beat, muscles quivering, she struggled to remember what had sent her into panic.

"*We*...you said *we*."

His arm rigid around her, his warm breath brushing her cheek, he studied her with an infuriating calm. "*Si.*"

Panic fluttered in her belly. "Why?"

"I'm coming with you."

"To Milan?"

"To New York."

Her gut flopped to her feet, leaving her hollow.

But his gaze remained serious.

Alex shook her head as if the action could bring her teetering world back to balance. "I don't understand."

Tapered fingers tightened over her slender wrist. Even in the sensual fog her senses waded through, Alex wondered if that was the true marker of his mood. "I wish to avoid the bother of calling you later, making an appointment, intruding on your busy life, dragging us all through the whole process again. With my forthcoming wedding and an irate fiancée to appease, it is better to get this out of the way."

"Get what out of the way?" she whispered.

Hardness edged in with the casual amusement in the narrow line of his mouth. "Meeting my daughter."

He'd shocked her.

A feral kind of thrill fizzed through Leandro's veins. Childish and uncharacteristic of him, he knew, but then, Alexis always brought out a side of him that he didn't know existed.

The longer she stared at him with that resolute light in her eyes, the sharper his awareness of his own desires became.

Elemental heat arose in him, his fingers tingling at the soft musculature of her belly, drenching him in remembered pleasure.

Last night, he'd been in shock. With a clear view of his plan this morning, the effect of Alexis's lush, understated beauty was stringent.

Her clean lemon soap scent lingered in his nostrils, more evocative than the most intrinsic perfume, provoking an overwhelming urge to bury his nose in the crook of her neck.

The neat braid she'd weaved her hair into made the scar stand out starkly against her pale brow.

Slender shoulders still held that battle-ready rigidity even though the way she had folded her arms and created distance between them, betrayed her.

Betrayed what though, Leandro had no idea. And that, he didn't like.

Her fierce stubbornness, her unerring resolve fascinated and frustrated him in equal measure.

Any other woman of his acquaintance would have shredded him in front of the curious guests, or lost a bit of that composure at being told that the man she'd dallied with long ago, the man who was the father of her child was engaged to be married.

Not Alexis.

The only time she'd lost her control had been at Antonio's disgusting words.

She was not the girl he had kissed so violently that night. On the cusp of womanhood, that Alexis had been an open canvas, her unflinching attraction to him utterly arousing, her languid, interested glances without artifice.

A temptation he'd failed to resist.

Now, this woman who faced him so calmly, so unwavering in her plans for *his role in their daughter's life*, without betraying the merest thought, even the merest hint of reaction at seeing him after all these years…she was a mystery.

Which meant he couldn't betray his hand either.

Only now, at the thought of him accompanying her, at his changing his plans, did she show a reaction.

"You look very pale, Alexis. Is something wrong?" he probed softly.

"It's not necessary that you come immediately," she said sharply. The T-shirt that he'd had the staff deliver hugged her round breasts as her chest fell and rose. "I mean, it's not a quick drive away and I can only imagine how…" she cast a glance behind her, as she continued, "occupied you must be with everything."

"Let me understand this. Are you discouraging me now?"

"No, I just…" Her unease was written in her pinched mouth.

Dark shadows cradled her brown eyes, and tenderness he didn't want to feel pierced Leandro.

He hadn't noticed it last night, but today he saw it clearly.

She was a wreck physically. That same instinct that had driven him to hold his brother and sister through the knocks they'd received, rode him now to hold her.

Fisting his hands, he waited for the urge to pass.

She wasn't his to care for.

"Is this not why you came? So that I could acknowledge Isabella and give you security about her future and then we continue in our merry ways?" Somehow, he managed to sound disinterested and unemotional at the whole prospect.

The pinched look instantly faded from her face. And Leandro had the answer to the question hadn't quite known to ask.

She wasn't going to fall in with his plans easily.

"Of course it is," she managed with a polite smile and walked away.

"This sneaky subterfuge is unlike you," Luca said at his side. Contempt sharpened his brother's usually laid-back tone. "Anyone who knows you can guess your intentions."

"Alexis does not." Trust his reckless brother to make him defensive.

"I would argue that she probably knows the true you,"

Luca smoothly interjected. "The man beneath the saint's skin."

Leandro flinched. The specter of his behavior toward Alexis seven years ago loomed large and loud in his mind. Demanding explanation and insight that he didn't want to give it. "If you expect elaboration on the event of seven years ago, no."

Scowling, Luca faced him. "*Event of seven years ago...* can you hear yourself? You seduced an innocent, and apparently, kicked her out the moment you zipped up. That is expected of me, not you."

Leandro cursed violently, Luca's crude words piercing him. Despite knowing that that's what Luca intended.

Innocent—that's what Alexis had been. And without meaning to, she had wielded it so well.

"Knowing the state you were in," Luca was relentless, saying, "you shouldn't have touched her."

"I know that."

"You used her, plain and simple."

Just like our father, his unsaid accusation hung heavy in the air. For Luca loathed even mentioning their father's name.

"*No,*" his hoarse refusal rang in the silence. He saw Alexis tense at the balcony and gritted his teeth. "I never made any false promises to her. *Cristo*, I didn't even..."

He couldn't put into words how alive he had felt every time Alexis had looked at him with those innocent brown eyes. How acute and agonizing the thrill had been when he touched her.

How much he'd needed to be needed, wanted like that after Rosa's death. Only when he had seen the look in her eyes had he realized how much he craved to lose himself.

How vulnerable he'd been in the face of such honest attraction as hers.

Not her, him.

He'd been the vulnerable one, he'd been the one who'd been seduced so easily and she hadn't even been trying.

No, even if he found the words, he couldn't tell Luca.

It was much too private, much too raw. Just remembering that night—the out-of-control, desperate desire, the stingingly sharp awareness made his muscles curl in memory. "It was not as dirty as you make it out to be, Luca."

"It seems so from where I stand. And from where she does, more importantly. She's the mother of your child, Leandro. At least now, treat her with respect. Aren't you the one always carping about the Conti legacy?

"Do not continue what he started, do not let this become our legacy."

Last night had been shock. Today, shame pounded through him. His whole life, he'd never treated another person, man or woman, the way he had Alexis.

All because first he'd weakened and then walked away from the consequences.

The very same traits that he'd despised in the man who'd fathered Luca and him.

"Whatever poison Antonio might spout, tell me you don't distrust her motives?"

"I trust every word she said last night." The thing that had kept him up all night was how telling what Alexis *hadn't* said was.

Last night and this morning...

If only she'd betrayed a spark of jealousy, or insecurity, if only she was like any other woman he'd known who would have thrown a reckless tantrum in the situation he'd put her in...*but no!*

Even then, he'd known she was different. Even then, he'd known the core of steel she possessed beneath that innocence.

And what an enticing contrast it made...

Which was also why he'd been so violently attracted to

her, a voice whispered. Why he had reached out to her in a way he hadn't done even with Rosa.

"Then you deceive her on purpose. You have Salvatore dangling on the line like a dog, Antonio threatening to hurt Valentina—"

"Will you marry Sophia Rossi then, Luca? Will you take her off my hands so that I don't worry about Valentina and can focus on my daughter instead?"

Luca's stinging silence was answer enough.

"Trust me," Leandro gritted through his teeth. "I'm ensuring that I do right by everyone involved."

"And her, Leandro? What about Alexis?"

Leandro ran a hand over his nape. What was right and what he wanted instead had always diverged when it came to this woman. And that he couldn't immediately seize control of the whole situation, that he couldn't make it right by any means available to him had kept him pacing to the first light of dawn.

He'd always thrived on being in control—of himself and his emotions and his situations, to beat circumstances into creating peace.

He and Luca and later, Valentina, wouldn't have found peace or even the merest happiness if he hadn't been able to count on his emotional invulnerability.

But Alexis, *then and now*, made him flounder like an impulsive, hormone-driven teenager.

"She has nothing to fear from me."

His brother's silence sent the most irrational surge of unease through him. Luca had the wickedest sense of humor Leandro had ever known. Not to mention carefree charm and the knack of making everyone feel at ease with him. Everything Leandro lacked and had never coveted.

Dio, he was thirty-five. Too late to acquire new qualities or affect a personality change. Not to mention he wouldn't be of use to his family if he did.

"Stay away from her, Luca. Your *particular brand* of friendship will only make it harder for me to—"

A roaring laugh fell from his brother's lips. "You know better than to wave a warning in my face. Also how I like to even the scales."

"This is far too important to me." He wanted to growl at his brother like an animal, he wanted to banish Luca to some Neverland until he had it all sorted with Alexis.

The thought of losing a daughter now that he'd found her was unacceptable.

"Then why not tell her that? Why not put your cards on the table?" Luca countered.

"You think she'll meekly agree to what I want after my behavior in the past?" Leandro said softly as Alexis came down the stairs and waited at a distance for Luca and him to finish talking. "Or would you instead advise me to take the small place she offers in my own daughter's life?

"Alexis is unlike any woman you or I have ever known."

For the first time since the blasted conversation began, Luca smiled that trademark devilish smile of his. Wide and reckless, his gaze took in Leandro leisurely, right down to his fisted hands.

Leandro had never, in his thirty-five years, felt the urge to punch the smile off his brother's face as he did then.

"Your saintly nature could stand to be tested now and then, Leandro."

While Leandro fumed in silence, and awash in an increasingly frequent stinging bitterness in his throat, his reckless brother reached her and enfolded Alexis in his arms, kissed her cheeks, made excited sounds over the picture of Isabella on her phone and whispered God knew what with that easy camaraderie Leandro would never achieve with her.

Nor did he need to, he assured himself.

CHAPTER FOUR

IT TOOK ALEX almost half the duration of the long flight to New York to get her head screwed on normally again. Between the flight, her headache and the effect Leandro had on her, she was going to have a nervous breakdown soon.

On top of the shock that he was coming with her had been the private airstrip the tinted-windowed Maserati had dropped them off at.

No uncomfortable economy seating purchased on Cheap-O-Fare for Leandro Conti or painfully long stopovers. The sleek Lear jet with its beige-and-black interior and wide, reclining-like-a-bed seats, the barely discernible hum as they took off had numbed her senses for a long while.

In lieu of this spectacular reminder of his wealth, all she'd been able to think of was what it said about him that he'd readily believed that she wasn't after his money.

He'd claimed to believe her seven years ago, too. Then why dismiss her so cruelly? Why hadn't he returned a single phone call?

I have to work, he'd told her once they had taken off, his mind clearly on other matters. He'd been on several calls since then, his attention on his laptop, Alex easily dismissed.

As always, a small resentful voice whispered. But then, there had never been anything remarkable about her, had there?

But once she'd settled in for the long flight, unease fluttered down her spine like a line of ants. It was clear that he'd postponed or canceled several meetings for this trip. Not to mention leaving his new fiancée behind, whose name she'd heard him mention more than once on his phone calls.

His actions didn't speak of a man who wanted to get an unwanted, distasteful complication out of the way so that he could go back to his pleasant life. Even as he'd claimed that was exactly why.

The continual, round-and-round, inconclusive thoughts all focused on the one man who'd always remained hurtfully elusive to her understanding on the heels of another sleepless night and the stress of the past few weeks made Alex's head pound in earnest.

Leaning her head back, she pressed her fingers onto her temples.

"Alexis, are you unwell?"

"I'm fine." Prickly, defensive and far too revealing than she wanted.

"Are we at war, *bella*? Because if so, I would like some notice."

The crisp scent of the ocean filled her nostrils and her eyes flicked open. He stood behind her seat, tall and broad, filling her vision. The stark, intensely masculine lines of his face were a sensual feast.

Before she could say no, his long fingers descended on her temples. "Here?"

His touch was cold.

Or was her skin unbearably hot?

With feathery lightness, he traced the width and length of the scar and the rucked tissue, again and again.

"Did they say if this would heal completely?"

"Years for the scar to disappear. I could have a skin graft, they said." She closed her eyes. "But I decided against it."

"You would rather bear the scar to remind you what you almost lost?"

Heart thudding at his perceptiveness, Alexis nodded weakly.

Her parents, even her friend Emma thought she should have the graft done. Put the accident behind her and move on. Count her blessings, they'd said.

She did count her blessings, but she wasn't the same person anymore. Whether in a good way or not, she didn't know.

Yet Leandro understood her so easily. "My mom thought it ruined my face," she said, hating herself for the insecurity she couldn't seem to squash.

Fingers resting on her chin, he tilted her up to face him. Amusement glittered in his eyes. Yet Alex didn't think he was laughing at her. "I didn't think you were the type to angle for a compliment."

"I'm not angling. I'm asking," she said, cursing the stubborn man.

Fingers tracing her cheekbones up and down, he tilted her face up so that she looked right into his eyes. His gaze touched her forehead, her brows, eyes, nose, mouth, chin, and swept upward again. "The scar detracts nothing from what beauty you possess, Alexis."

A curse flew from her mouth then. God, the man couldn't even hand out a pity compliment, could he?

"I hope you don't speak like that in front of Isabella."

"Did anyone tell you you're an arrogant jackass, Leandro?"

Amusement sharpened those cheeks of his. "Luca does, quite frequently. Although I have to say it feels especially satisfactory to hear it from your mouth, Alexis."

She was still struggling with that when his fingers moved over her forehead again, quick and firm, exerting just the right amount of pressure.

She groaned at the sweet relief, the sound wrenching from the depths of her. It was no different from the nurse or doctors who had checked her relentlessly those first few weeks after the accident, she tried to convince herself.

"Thanks." She held his wrists, intending to push him away. And felt muscled sinew, the hair rasping against her palm. Innocent touch turned to searing awareness in a breath. "I'm okay now."

When he spoke, steel edged his silky, smooth tone. "Alexis, if you tell me where it hurts precisely and why you whimper with such pain, then maybe I can relieve it a little. If you, however, insist on this prickly attitude, I will touch and prod you everywhere until I can figure it out. And I'm sure neither of us wants that."

"I haven't been sleeping well," she added quickly, "and it's all catching up with me. It feels like someone's taking a sledgehammer inside my head."

"Relax now," he commanded in that voice of his.

As if she could ever relax in his presence. As if that relentless peal of her nerves could ever quiet.

She had no knowledge of how long he was at it, but *God*, the man could weave magic with those fingers. In more than one way if her memories were right.

Welcome heat streaked through her temples as his clever fingers pressed just the right amount in the perfect rhythm at all the right places. Up and down, back and forth. Faster and harder. "You're really good at this," she pointed out, her voice hoarse.

"Luca always had the worst kind of headaches growing up. He would…be at the piano for days, inhales books on so many different subjects, not sleep through nights at a time, then have raging headaches for days after. It was hard to watch him struggle with it so I learned a few techniques to ease it."

Every time his fingers swooped down over her nape,

sparks tingled. Languor filled her blood. "Where were your parents?" she asked and then realized she'd never heard any of the siblings mention them. Then or now.

"My father was not fit to be called one, much less a decent human being, and our mother," his voice tempered here, "for years, she had her own problems."

"What about Antonio?"

"Antonio is old-school. He thought Luca was pretending for attention and told him to toughen up."

"You didn't?" she asked, her curiosity flaming. Not that it had ever been dormant when it came to this man.

"I knew how much Luca suffered, for all the outrageous tricks he played. I had to do something."

She opened her eyes and found the penetrating gray of his. Neck stretched over the leather seat, there was nowhere else for her gaze to land.

The white collar of his shirt was a stark contrast against the dark skin of his throat. He would feel like tempered steel and rough silk, she knew, her fingers curling around the hand rest.

Without the formal clothes, he should have looked more attainable. He didn't. It was the confidence in his eyes, the sense of authority that clung to him like a second skin.

He seemed as out of her orbit as he'd been seven years ago.

"How old were you?" She somehow managed to get back on track.

"Fourteen."

Fourteen years old and he'd been so thoughtful about his brother's pain.

Another small facet of his personality and yet all Alex felt was like she was tunneling through darkness. Her relentless awareness of his masculinity and his shabby treatment of her seven years ago only counted against him.

"Tell me about the accident," he prodded softly.

He peppered her with specific questions, asking for numerous details, about her injuries, recovery period, right down to the names of the nurses who'd attended her.

With her muscles turning into mush, Alex gave over to his deep voice, and those magical hands. Told him of the weeks she spent in the hospital, seeing Izzie's face burst into tears at the sight of her in the stark bed, of wondering if she'd have use of her hand again.

"Your hand?" He walked around her seat immediately. "What happened to your hand?"

He lifted her left hand in his bigger one and studied the crisscross of scars across the puckered skin in the back. The pithy curse that fell from his mouth almost distracted her from the gentle, almost reverent touch.

Bluntly cut square nails. Long, tapered fingers. Rough calluses. She studied his hands to her heart's content. He traced the veins on the back of her hand, sending a tingle up her arm.

"It got crushed in the impact. The nerve damage was far too extensive. But they said continued physical therapy will help."

She tried to pull her hand away, suddenly feeling self-conscious. But he didn't let go. "Was that the hardest part?"

Alexis looked down at their joined hands, her throat swelling. With his soothing tone and gentle caresses, he made her long for something that she couldn't even define.

The worst offender was mistaking that she interested him. That he was as aware of her as she was of him.

"The hospital food."

A soft smile curved his mouth, changing the entire vista of his forbidding features. Like one ray of sunlight that pierced even the thickest, densest darkness.

A carefree, laughing Leandro.

It was as novel as it was attractive. Even back then, her first impression of him had been how serious he was.

"Is Isabella like you? Strong and stubborn?"

Smiling, she nodded. "Actually, the hardest part was the sheer amount of insurance paperwork that I had to deal with. But Justin was a great help with that."

It was like she'd seen the show about predators on National Geographic. Just an infinitesimal tightening of those features—head cocking, muscles bunching in his shoulders. Regrouping before attacking. "Who is Justin?" He didn't quite meet her gaze.

"He's my friend Emma's brother. Moved back last year."

"A good friend then?"

Something in his tone tugged but the pounding in her head easing, Alex couldn't care. "We've been on a few dates this past year," she said, thinking back on how strange it had been to step out without Izzie. How hard it had been to accept Justin's help knowing that he liked her and she…she didn't feel anything like that about him.

Having known Justin for a long time, her parents, however, had all but started planning their wedding.

"A boyfriend then?" He stood up and moved behind her again, his hands moving to her head again as if they had never left.

When she looked up at him, a frown marred his brow. "Izzie likes him, too," she said, parroting her mother.

"And you, Alexis? Do you like him?" The question was silky smooth but the speed with which he asked made her heart race.

"It's hard to not like Justin. Especially when I found last year how quickly men run in the opposite direction because I come with a child in tow."

"What do you mean?"

"Emma decided I needed to get back out there and took out an ad on *Forever.com*. Forget *forever*, apparently, being a single mom means I don't even get a first date. This one creep who did contact me said it's good to have proof that I was fertile." She cringed. "Fortunately, Justin proved I wasn't quite as plague-ridden for men as I thought."

"You miss excitement in your life then?"

"Will you count it against me in this test if I say yes?" she said teasingly.

"A test?" He sounded so innocent that she laughed. "To what end?"

"To gauge my credibility as a mother and guardian before you settle money on Izzie?"

He did really laugh then. It was a deep, husky sound that wrapped around Alex like a warm blanket. "That is a cynical statement. Even an insult, I think, as it implies I care more about my money than a newly discovered daughter."

"I didn't say that," she pointed out. "I have no idea what kind of man you are, Leandro. Except for how you treated me. So if there's an insult here and there in the way I speak to you, then it's not intended."

"Then we have to learn about each other."

"Do we? Will you answer anything I ask of you?"

He smiled again and it stole through Alexis, warming her up from the inside, infusing her with a deep sense of well-being. Like one of Izzie's sweet and tight cuddles. Like the smell of the first cup of coffee in the morning. Like the crisply cold air in Central Park after a night's snowfall in winter.

"Are you bracing me with that question or yourself?"

How did he see through her so easily?

She was still chewing on that when he spoke. "Has it been hard? Doing it all on your own?"

Tension, she didn't know from where, swirled in the air all of a sudden. A million answers crowded in on her and Alex held her breath.

"For as long as I can remember, I worried about Luca

and then Valentina." Deep and low, his voice washed over her. But even more shocking was how readily he spoke of his past. "Still, only about their mental health and happiness. Not actual tangible things like their safety, finances and other things. Not to mention—"

"But that sounds like you had to grow up too fast."

He shrugged. Clearly, he hadn't seen it as a loss. "I did what anyone would have done. I could not let Luca or Valentina suffer my parents' negligence."

"Don't you regret that you missed out on a carefree, reckless kind of childhood then?"

Whatever reply came to him, he cut it off and looked down at her. "You sound wistful, Alexis. Are you sorry that you haven't lived recklessly enough?"

Pure taunt sizzled in that question.

He was thinking about that night, Alexis knew as surely as the pulsing beat of her heart. "Or the fact that having Isabella curtails you from it now?"

Refusing to take his bait, Alex looked away. Her confusion about him only rose. Made worse by her stringent awareness of him.

He'd looked after his brother and sister since he'd been a teenager. Even that week in Italy, he'd come to the villa because Valentina had slipped on some steps and twisted her ankle.

Within an hour, there he'd been—a hauntingly beautiful and masculine figure, concerned about his sister.

"Before the accident," she said, trying to cover up her confusion, "it was more a sense of never having a moment to breathe. If it wasn't the day-to-day things at the store, it was Izzie getting sick. If it wasn't Izzie, it was some health issue with my dad. If it wasn't him, then wondering about finances…" She pulled in a deep breath. "After the accident though, yes, it felt hard. And not just because of the panic attacks."

"Panic attacks? Has Isabella seen you have one?"

That he immediately thought of Izzie both warmed and alarmed Alex. "No, she hasn't. It's just fragments from the accident, that sense of my life careening out of control. I had them only a couple of times but they made me determined to ensure Izzie's future."

Not even with Emma had she admitted how much it had all become for her before the accident. And yet, sharing bits and pieces from his own past, Leandro had put her instantly at ease.

It was almost as if he'd decided to make peace with her. Did he think they could forge a friendship of some sort? Would they be like those amicable partners who shared a child?

Because as good as that sounded ideally, Alex couldn't fool herself that she could ever be just friends with Leandro. Not if she wanted to remain sane.

Even now, headache relieved, a sleepy, languorous flush claimed her.

Her jacket off her shoulders, she was awash in pure, skittering sensation.

Then those supple fingers stole under her T-shirt, pushed under the straps of her bra and pressed into the knots in her shoulders. Alex groaned, every inch of her thrumming in a molten kind of way.

It had been so long since she'd been touched by such strong, masculine hands that made her aware of her own fragility.

A desperate yearning took hold of her. She turned her cheek toward the rough hand. Rubbed it against the hair-roughened wrist. Shivers spewed everywhere.

She could just imagine those hands everywhere on her skin, teasing, taunting, drenching her in—

The utter stillness of his form, the rough texture of his

hand against her cheek, so incredibly good and yet so alien, jerked Alex back into coherence.

Breath hitching in and out roughly, she pushed off her seat.

Skin tight over angular features, Leandro stared back at her. Not a smidgen of the confusion or the stringent awareness that vibrated through every inch of her reflected in his own gaze however.

"Thanks," she said jerkily, wrapping her hands around herself. "I'm…much better."

"Are you in love with this… Justin, Alexis?" he said, without heeding the distance she'd put between them.

Senses still raw from the sensations coursing through her, shocked at how much she wanted his hands on her, a choked breath fell from her lips. The resolute lift of his chin, the implacable look in his eyes…that pushed his question to sink through. "You think I came to Italy because I'm hitching up with a man and want to fob off Izzie on you?"

Jaw tight, he wrapped his fingers around her wrist and tugged her closer. "No. As shocking as it is, it seems you're an exceptional mother and—"

Oh, the man made her so mad. "Why is it so shocking? That I had sex with you and liked it makes it impossible that I'm also a good mother? If that's the kind of attitude you're going to show around Izzie about her mother—"

He covered her mouth with his palm. Thoughts fragmented. Sensation zoomed. It was heat all over, stinging, unrelenting. From his palm, from his lean frame standing so close to her. Beneath her skin, in her muscles.

"I would never disrespect her mother in front of Isabella. And I said it the wrong way."

"Your timing sucks, that's what Valentina said to me." She had been so keen upon the previous night, she hadn't realized what that meant. "Seven years ago and now. With you…what did she mean? What was going on when we met seven years ago?"

"It is irrelevant, Alexis."

"To me, you mean?" she instantly challenged him, head cocked. "Way to put me in my place, Leandro. But this stopped being about me and you six years ago."

The question about seven years ago was a sharp reminder to Leandro of how easily Alex could distract him. Of how easily one innocent touch could morph into this craving.

"My wife had—"

Alex clutched his shirt, her knees threatening to give out under her. "*Your wife…* God, you were married?"

"*No!* I would never… No, she had passed away recently when we…met."

"How recently?"

"A month to the day that night."

A month…the leaden weight on her chest eased enough for her to breathe.

Until she met his gaze, saw the self-loathing that settled into every line of his face.

"Rosa died after a long struggle with cancer and it took me mere weeks to forget that."

Shame crawled through her insidiously, polluting her memory of that night, painting her with that same loathing she heard in his voice.

She pressed the heels of her hands to her eyes. *God, why had she asked?* "If you were the bloody saint your sister calls you, you shouldn't have come near me, you shouldn't have touched me."

"You think I didn't try?" He dragged her to him in a violent explosion of temper. "From the moment I laid eyes on you… *Maledizione!*" Fingers dug into her arms. Hard chest grazed her breasts. Her body came awake as if someone had thumped on her heart.

Excruciatingly, violently awake.

The hard length of his legs cradled hers, shaping and molding her muscles. "From the moment I saw you telling Tina not to be a spoiled, whiny brat, from the moment I saw you laugh with Luca…your face…*you haunted me*." Fingers splayed over her jaw, he caressed every inch of her face with his eyes.

Was he remembering or did he still want her?

"Rosa suffered with cancer for three years. Through endless chemo cycles, I never even looked at another woman. I never even felt the urge.

"But every time I looked at you, there it was in your eyes. Your attraction to me, so guileless, so honest… The more I tried to stay away from the villa, the more times I found myself there. The more I told myself to leave you alone, the more I found myself near you."

Leave it alone, Alex. Every self-preserving instinct yelled at her. But she didn't heed it. "So you're saying that I asked to be hurt? That I didn't deserve a speck of the respect that you had for your wife? That I deserved to be slept with and then discarded—"

He covered her mouth with his finger. "There was no future for us. *There was no us.* Not even an affair. I did what I did to make sure you understood that."

"I would've preferred knowing that you weren't a heartless, ruthless jerk who used women and then abhorred them for wanting the same as you. I would've preferred to be treated as a person.

"I would have preferred knowing that you were grieving, that you—"

"*No*, Alexis! Do not spin theories about me. Do not make me out to be anything more than I am."

"Your arrogance in dictating to me what I should think of you is astounding, Leandro." She faced him, her heart pounding. "What scares you so much? That I might think you're a man with a conscience? That I might think you liked me and that you wanted me that night as much as I did you? That there was a connection between us that threatened all your principles?"

A muscle jumped in his clamped jaw. His head cocked, infinitesimally, as if something had come at him.

Gaze absolutely implacable, he looked at her. Slowly, Alex could see any hint of emotion driven out by his sheer, ruthless will. Could see the man of the past few hours retreat. Could feel the intangible wall rise up between them.

A shiver climbed up her spine. Like a warning to brace herself.

"What I did that night was a betrayal to Rosa. I obviously misjudged the effect of prolonged celibacy, especially when thrown in front of an irresistible temptation. I saw her waste away month after month and you…you were everything she couldn't be at the end.

"Vivacious, lively, beautiful.

"To hold you, to touch you…it's like that shot that shocks the heart." He closed his eyes, every line of his face taut. "It was pure animal lust, nothing civilized, nothing to build something on. If it wasn't you, I'm perfectly sure it would have been someone else soon."

The moment the words were out of his mouth, Leandro knew it was the utterly wrong thing to have said for the goal he had in mind.

Color leeched from her skin, leaving Alexis's features pinched. Like the lights going out of a brilliantly lit room.

Dio, the woman turned him inside out. He had destroyed his entire strategy of putting her at ease, of showing that he could be understanding and perceptive, of earning her trust with his words.

What did she want—to elevate one night of weakness to life-changing import?

No!

He couldn't let her weave fantasies about that night, couldn't risk letting her imagine romantic ideas about the future. Not the kind she obviously still believed in, even after he'd behaved like a ruthless bastard.

He was exactly what she thought him—heartless, arrogant, used to getting his own way.

Still, she held her head high and faced him square, didn't buck against his obviously cruel summation of that night.

"Will you look at Izzie like she was a symbol of your betrayal, too? Because I swear, Leandro—" She looked ferociously breathtaking, eyes flashing fire. "I won't let you come near her if you do."

Rendered mute, Leandro stared at her, amazed by the strength she showed even now.

What would it be like to possess a woman like her? To have her channel that intensity, that passion toward him? To bask in the strength of her conviction?

If his mother had possessed half that strength, would he have turned out different? Would he have had that reckless, carefree childhood that Alex mourned for him? Would he have known tender feelings?

Would he—

Dio! It was as useless as it was pathetically self-indulgent.

He was the man he was, for better or worse. But she deserved an explanation. "For years, Rosa wanted a child and we didn't conceive. When you told me about Isabella, all I could think of was her. Of how cruel it was, even to her memory that I had a child with a woman I took in a moment of insanity.

"I would never hold an innocent responsible for my lack of judgment."

Chin lifted. Shoulders squared. She had never looked so

icily cold as she did then. Whatever inner fire that made her Alexis seemed to go out of her eyes.

He felt a moment's regret about what was right for her. But like she had said, this wasn't about either of them anymore.

"No, only me, because I was a willing participant in your betrayal. Thanks for clearing that up."

She left the main cabin like a queen who had found him wanting.

It rattled him how much he wanted to follow her. How much he wanted to take her in his arms and tell her that all his disgust had been aimed at himself. That he considered her an innocent in all of this, too. That as much as he'd loathed himself, *Dio*, he'd never been able to forget her.

Even today, his self-control, his very intention in all this was threatened by all the things she made him feel.

But, at least this way, she would know what she was getting.

Because, as much as he resisted, there was only one way to be a part of his daughter's life.

He'd been prepared to marry Sophia. One woman was the same as another for the marriage he wanted. Of course, he could have lied and made his goal easier, but Leandro didn't believe in pretending things he didn't feel.

CHAPTER FIVE

FROM THE MOMENT he realized he had a daughter, Leandro had tried to imagine what he would feel a thousand times. After all, he had raised Valentina for all intents and purposes. Something novel from the emotional spectrum he'd ever experienced, he admitted that much.

But the sight of the little girl that barely came to his knees, looking up at him with those gray eyes, both curious and reticent, punched through him. It was as if he was caught in a whirlpool of emotion, tossed about by a vicious eddy that threw him from grief to anger to sheer, gut-wrenching amazement that she was his.

And loss, excruciating loss.

It had been almost close to an hour since he and Alexis had arrived at the tiny brownstone house that belonged to her parents.

Tension swirled through the air from the moment she introduced him. The Sharpes were too polite to say anything to his face, better than what Alexis had received back in his home, but their doubt filled the air. Even more powerful was their obvious anger for Alexis. She had forgotten to mention that she had come to see him against their wishes.

After an excruciatingly uncomfortable half hour, they went to visit with friends and Leandro had been able to breathe again.

Keeping to his word, he had held himself back from approaching Isabella.

But waiting had never felt so painful as he heard Alexis's firm but husky tone and Isabella's soft voice in the kitchen. He had no one to blame. Neither would he let anything nor anyone stop him from setting it to right.

He stayed on the couch, anxious like never before when Alexis and Isabella walked back into the tiny living area.

Reaching him, Isabella leveled an unabashedly curious look at him. "Mamma says you're my *papà*."

Leandro cleared his throat, found himself unable to utter a word still. Chill and heat, everything enveloped him.

"She said you guys were friends before and then fell out. Is that why you didn't come to see me before?" His gaze flew to Alexis's and held. That she hadn't filled his daughter's head with anything but the truth made his own treatment of her even more awful. "It's okay," Isabella continued, laying her small hand upon his. "My friend Sam and I fight all the time, too. Mamma says friends gotta make up after fights. You and Mamma made up?"

"*Si*...yes," he corrected himself when he saw her little frown. "We have."

"Does that mean I can tell my friends that you'll be—?"

"Izzie, sweetie," Alexis interrupted, "remember how we talked about your *papà* living all the way in Italy and us—"

"You can tell all your friends, Isabella," Leandro added, ignoring Alexis's pursed mouth. "Maybe we can even meet your friend Sam tomorrow? Would you like that?"

"Can we throw the ball around with them? Sam's dad has a really good arm."

Even as his arms ached to pull her into his embrace, even as prickling heat knocked at his eyes, Leandro consoled himself with shaking his little girl's hand. "*Si*, we can. Although it is your uncle, Luca, who's the best with a ball in the family."

A cute, heart-wrenching smile split her mouth. And Leandro's breath caught.

It was in Isabella's smile that Alexis peeked through. The effervescent joy, the confident tilt of the chin, the way it tore through him… Alexis was in his daughter where it mattered. "I have an uncle?"

"You have an uncle, an aunt and a great-*nonno* in Italy, who're all dying to meet you."

"What's a *nonno*?" Before he could answer, she tugged his hand. "Can I show you my new puzzle? Are you going to stay here? We only have three bedrooms but you can have mine. Unless you want to sleep in Mamma's room now that you're friends again?"

He laughed as her questions continued, much like the machine that threw tennis balls at a player.

"No, sweet pie, he can't stay here."

"Why not?" Both he and Isabella asked at the same time.

Alexis's smile didn't falter. "Our house is too small for you. But Brooklyn has luxury hotels that should suit your exacting tastes."

"I'm staying here, Alexis."

His heart threatening to burst out of his chest, Leandro stood up and followed his little girl to her room.

Even as he was aware of a set of molten brown eyes digging into his back, censure and curiosity and a million other questions in them.

Maybe taking Izzie on a holiday to Italy for the summer isn't such a bad idea, Alex. Izzie will get to meet the Contis and you can have a nice break.

Her dad's words from this morning still rumbled through Alex, like the after-ripples of an earthquake that had upended her world this morning.

You went when we warned you against it. Now that he's being so reasonable, what's bothering you?

This was her mother. Clenching her teeth so hard that

her jaw hurt, Alex dragged another cardboard box with canned organic beans.

The damning thing was the heartless, manipulative jerk hadn't even broached the subject of visiting Italy with her. Yet, here was her dad, the very man who'd looked at Leandro with the utmost suspicion last week, persuading her to not hold grudges and do what was best for Izzie.

Even now, her throat burned at her parents' continual, insidious hints about Leandro being a model father to Izzie. While they had never approved of a single decision of hers.

How had he done that? In just two weeks, how had he turned her own parents and even her best friend against her? And to what end?

Also, why was the man who'd wanted to be on his merry way to his waiting fiancée still here?

Marking off the cans on her inventory chart, Alex blew out a long breath. The broken A/C in the beginning of a New York summer meant the storeroom was like a sauna. Sweat poured in rivulets down the back of her neck. With her hospital bills from the myriad of treatments she had undergone still arriving every few weeks like buzzards circling a dead body, she couldn't afford to get the air-conditioning fixed now. Nor could she hire extra help to sort and stock their inventory.

Cursing, she pulled her cotton T-shirt off her back. The damn thing went straight back to sticking to her skin. Making sure that she didn't put undue strain on her left hand, she knelt in front of another box and ripped off the duct tape. She knew she was pushing herself, that this inventory could wait until next week after the long hours she had put in over the past few days.

God, she'd barely even spent any time with Izzie.

But going back home before she was exhausted meant seeing the blasted man. Seeing him meant remembering his words from the flight. Remembering meant…realizing that she'd, foolishly, hoped he would have some magnanimous reason for his behavior seven years ago. How naively unsophisticated she was in not accepting that she'd been a convenient lay and nothing else.

Until he'd said the words, until they had landed on her like poisonous darts, Alex didn't know they'd hurt so much. Didn't know that they would make her want to burrow into an emotional shell like Izzie's pet turtle and never emerge.

He'd been devoted to his wife, Alexis couldn't get over that. It said everything she'd assumed about him was wrong. Exactly opposite even.

Only when she saw him and Izzie together—Leandro, powerful and handsome and so thoroughly masculine and Izzie, tiny and smiling and his very image—did she remember the reason he was here.

Knowing that he was sleeping in the bedroom next to hers made even the little sleep she'd been getting disappear.

He should've looked incongruous in the small bed in Izzie's room, yet he looked right at home. Just as he'd slipped so easily into the role of a father.

With his utter devotion to Izzie, with his unpretentious, get-your-hands-dirty gardening skills he'd helped her mom with, with his keen attention to several issues that had to be fixed in the house and immediately arranging workers to do so...

In her parents' view, suddenly the man had gone from dishonorable stranger who'd impregnated and then ditched their reckless, good-for-nothing daughter *and more importantly*, their much-adored granddaughter to an accomplished, down-to-earth-even-though-he's-stinking-rich gentleman who could do no wrong in their eyes.

If she didn't hate him before this, Alex was sure she did now.

She attacked the second line of the stubborn tape with both hands, her temper finally fraying.

"*Alexis!*" came the thunderous growl from behind her.

Before she could react, she was hauled up from behind, viselike hands clamped tight under her arms. Awareness smoldered through her, like a current of lightning.

The moment she was upright, his grip gentled. Long fingers rested on the upper curves of her breasts. Air burned through her lungs.

Her back felt as though it would bow from the pressure of holding herself stiff.

The sheer violence of her need to feel those fingers drift down, the instant tightening of her nipples hungry for his touch, ripped through her. One step back would send her into the hard, male muscle that every inch of her wanted to feel.

God, the man was engaged to another woman. Didn't her body understand that?

Longing made her throat burn, muscles quiver, skin thrum. She didn't dare wiggle for fear of him touching her. "Let me go, Leandro," she said in a husky voice. "I'm all sweaty."

Instead of heeding her, he took a step further. The blanket of heat that surrounded her was instantaneous. The scent of him drifted down over her skin, covering every cell. Drenching her until all she breathed was him. "Not until you tell me what, *per carita*, you are doing."

As always, he sounded perfectly balanced, unruffled.

"I'm working. We can't all dance attendance on you," she snapped, and then regretted her words.

When he tried to turn her, she resisted. She couldn't face him, feeling so raw and vulnerable. She couldn't face herself if she betrayed how much she still wanted him.

Closing her eyes, she willed her breath to calm.

"Should you be pulling and pushing boxes that weigh a ton when your hand is nowhere near healed?"

"I was careful to not use my left hand."

"And what if you hurt your other hand dragging things that shouldn't be handled without the appropriate tool?"

"I can take care of myself, Leandro."

A hiss of impatient breath. "That is not up for debate. But that there are numerous things you need help with is fact, too. Especially around the store."

"You forget that I've been taking care of my parents, Izzie and the store. We don't need your help. This isn't why I asked you to come."

She heard his muttering in Italian, before she turned and looked up at him.

The clean, strong lines of his face struck her with that same fierce hunger.

For the first time since she'd laid eyes on him again, he looked truly confounded. If she wasn't battling her hyper-awareness of him and her growing, irrational temper, she would've enjoyed the look on his face.

"Why are you always so defensive? I will say this again because it does not seem to enter your stubborn mind. I do not think that you came to see me for any reason other than Isabella's welfare. And I am…glad that you did. Any man who turns away from his duty is not worth the air he breathes.

"Now, I have instructed your father to call back the manager who used to assist him at the store but full-time. My real estate agent has had some interest in the store, too."

"For one thing, I can't afford to hire staff now." Alex gritted her jaw. "And I have no plans to sell the store."

He didn't even bat an eyelid. "I have transferred some money to your account. That should help until the store is completely operational again."

God, the man had to be the most thickheaded, arrogant, high-handed specimen of the species. Didn't he realize she wanted nothing to do with him on a personal level? That her pride, which was all she had at this point, was hanging by a sheer thread? "I'm not taking money from you."

"Why not?"

"Why should I?"

He looked at her as if she were lacking brains completely. "Because I have it and you need it."

"I don't know what the hell kind of game you're playing, or what you're trying to prove. Or is that it? You get a kick out of changing how my parents see you? Your monumental ego can't stand that they think less of the mighty Leandro Conti?"

"*Cristo*, I only intend to help you. You think I like knowing that you struggled so much all these years when I should have helped?"

The guilt in his eyes stayed her for a few seconds.

"Well, I don't want your help. Is it not enough that you… you own half your country, do you also have to be good at gardening and fixing the house and a million other things?" Didn't he see how hard he was making this all for her? "You might as well label me incompetent and be done with it."

If he had ever assumed he could understand the complexities of Alexis's mind, he was wrong. A simple conversation with her was like handling a hundred Lucas and Valentinas on their worst days.

From the moment they had spoken of that night seven years ago, it was as if there was an invisible wall between them and she had retreated behind it.

Except when they were both with Isabella. That was the only time she smiled, the only time she made eye contact with him.

Dio, the only time the stubborn woman even acknowledged his presence in her house.

He hadn't been there a single night before he realized how much responsibility rested on her shoulders, how many day-to-day things Alexis handled with barely a complaint and with an efficiency that he couldn't help but admire.

Still, it was too much for one person. She had handled so much for so long alone.

It had proved easy enough to win her parents over now that he truly intended to take care of Isabella and even Alexis by association, to change their perception that he was the big bad wolf that had gobbled up their lovely daughter.

Only Alexis began to act strange. The more her parents and even her friend Emma realized his true intentions and supported him, the more withdrawn she became. A betrayed look dawned in her gaze. Now, when he was finally doing the right thing.

And the worst thing was that her mistrust was taking a toll on him. The more she dismissed him, the more stringent became his need to make her acknowledge him, and his right to be in her life.

Not just his right over Isabella. But he wanted Alexis, too.

There it was...the knot that he hadn't been able to unravel in the past week.

Look at how he had held her just now. At how violently and instantly his body had reacted to the mere graze of her slender curves against his. At how insanely powerful the urge was to touch her, to taste her, to bury his nose in the crook of her neck and breathe in the scent of her skin.

His desire for her was already out of control, threatening his plan.

When her friend Justin had visited and embraced her, all

he'd wanted to do was pull her away from the young, blond, insufferably amiable giant and tuck her away behind him.

To declare like a Neanderthal that Alexis wasn't available.

When they had laughed together over some childhood story, when he'd seen how familiar Justin was with Alexis and everything regarding her…he'd felt the most absurd sense of jealousy.

He hadn't felt possessive even about a toy in his childhood.

Teeth clenched, eyes closed, he counted to ten.

The scent of her, skin and sweat and undeniably her, it filled his lungs, his blood, unlocking every rebellious, insidiously craven indulgence his body wanted with her.

Dio, how he wanted her. Even after everything. Even today.

She would be his wife, his to possess, his to protect.

She would be in his bed, his room, his life. He could have her whenever, wherever, however he wanted, until this madness in his blood was defeated. Until every irrationally possessive clawing was satisfied. Until he was inured to this feverish desire he felt for her.

Until he could look at her and feel nothing but satisfaction that he'd done the right thing.

Beneath this war she was waging with him, Alexis was like him. At such a young age, she'd been forced into being a mother and yet it was clear that she exceled at it. She cared for everyone around her, to the detriment of her own well-being.

Now, he would look after her. Just as he had done Rosa.

She would see how good of a father he could be and would want for nothing.

They could have a marriage without drama, without the messiness of emotions. By the time the attraction between them fizzled out, they would have more children.

And then they would be bound as parents who cared about their children.

Hadn't that been his only condition when Antonio had found Rosa for him? That his new bride be someone who would love their children and devote herself to being a calm, supportive wife?

Alexis needed his strength, just as Rosa had done, only in a different way. She needed to be protected from her stubborn self first.

Only with that promise did the clamoring hunger in his blood subside.

"Alexis," he said in a composed tone, "explain to me how offering help is calling you incompetent. How trying to reassure your parents that I mean well for Isabella is," he held himself back, just, from sounding possessive about her, knowing that it would only alienate her, "...wrong."

"That's exactly the problem." Chin tilted up, her gaze flashed fire at him. Her thin T-shirt hugged the round globes of her breasts. His hands itched to touch her, trace those lush curves, to mold them. Blood hummed with a thrum as he imagined baring her to his gaze.

"You've been here barely two weeks and they worship you. They love everything you do." A choked whimper escaped her, her mouth trembling. "It's almost as if everything I've tried to do for more than a decade counts for nothing." She threw the pad in her hand against the wall, her lithe form shaking. "It's almost as if I... I count for nothing."

The sheen of moisture in her eyes punched through him, tying his insides into a knot.

Tenderness like he'd never known assailed him, releasing the fist-like tension that had been driving him this past week. He'd always been protective of those around him. It was in his nature, in his blood. And yet, nothing unmanned him as much as Alexis's tears did.

The very defiance of her meeting his gaze even as those brown eyes welled up…it was a breath-stealing sight. He wished he could capture it on paper, or in a song, like Luca would have. He wished he had words to describe how magnificently beautiful she was.

Instead, he did the one thing he'd always exceled at.

His large hands on her slender shoulders, he pulled her to him and wrapped his arms around her. Even stiff and unbending as she was, she still came. That she took the comfort he offered told him how upset she was.

"Alexis." He had never tried so hard to sound understanding, never felt such raw impatience tearing at him to fix her grief. "Tell me what bothers you and I'll fix it."

Forehead resting against his chest, she let out a slow exhale. "For once, I can't hate your arrogance, Leandro. I'd give anything if you could fix it."

Smiling, he stroked her temples. "You don't know what I can do until you try me, *cara*. You haven't been sleeping again, have you?"

"I miss him." Teary and choked, she sounded unlike the Alexis he knew. "I miss him so much."

Such unparalleled love reverberated in her tone that everything within him stilled. "Who are you taking about?"

"You'll think me the most horrible person ever."

"When have you cared about my opinion, Alexis?" he shot back, hating the thread of disquiet that coursed through him.

Just as he expected, her spine straightened. That fighting spirit returned to her eyes. "I don't. I just… It's my brother, Adrian."

Relief was a palpable thing within him. A lover would have caused problems for him. That was the only reason for it. "I didn't know you had a brother."

"He died when I was seventeen, just before he was about to start college. Oh you'd have liked him so much.

He was charming, brilliant, handsome, kind…exceled at his studies, sports. *God*, there was nothing that Adrian wasn't good at.

"I could have hated him for being their favorite, if he hadn't loved me so much. You see, unlike Adrian, I didn't excel at anything. I barely got through my classes. Mom and Dad and I never really connected… Adrian was always the buffer. When he passed away suddenly…" She wiped her eyes with the heels of her hands, much like Isabella did. "Not only were we shattered, but it felt like there was nothing connecting me to them. There were days when I wished I had died instead of him."

"*Dio,* Alexis!" The very thought unnerved Leandro on so many levels. "I'm sure your parents didn't wish that."

"No, probably not." She stepped away from him. "I have tried my level best to be a good daughter. But I… I'm not him. Seeing how happy and elated they are with everything you do, how easy you make it all, I'm sure it reminds them of him. Of how different and how better life would've been if he were alive.

"And I can't be angry with them for thinking that because it's true. I drove a very fiscally wise store toward ruin with my ideas, got pregnant at twenty and…now, I brought a myriad of problems on us with this accident."

Cristo, didn't anyone tell her that all those were not her fault? That she was braver and stronger than any woman in the same situation? Didn't she realize it was her parents' fault in measuring her against a son who was long gone?

Leandro wanted to shake her and somehow show her the image he had of her.

But finally, he understood her behavior of the past week.

Alexis was used to taking care of everyone around her, of putting everyone else's needs first. In just a week, he'd seen her handle ten different things for her mother, Isabella and even her friend Emma.

It was time for someone to remove such weight from her shoulders. And he would do it. Even if he had to manipulate that very weakness of hers.

"A small business that you think you ruined in a hard, economic climate, accolades at university you think you lack, ambition you think you don't possess." He had heard all those insidious remarks from her mother, the regretful but equally hurting statements from her father, only the awareness that he would take her away from it all had stopped him from peeling their hide. "How do they measure up against the strong, happy little girl you've been raising all these years, Alexis? Against swallowing your anger for me and coming to me when you worried about Isabella's future? I would have given anything to see my mother champion for us like you do her."

Her stunned gaze, her mouth falling open soundlessly— her shock at his words was a tangible thing in the air. Something in his chest ached at how desperate she had been to hear a compliment. To be told that she wasn't a failure.

Her disbelief slowly ebbed out of her eyes. "I...don't know what to say."

"Learn to accept my help."

She swiped at her eyes with the back of her hand and glared at him. "So nothing I just told you got through to your head?"

"Whatever I'm doing, it's so that you can breathe easy when you come to Italy with me. So that you don't worry about the store or them. They deserve better than to worry about your health and Izzie's security and about what you'll do when they're gone. They deserve that holiday they've been planning for ages."

"How do you know about their trip to Australia?"

"Your mother showed me the brochure."

That same inadequacy swirled through Alex. How had

she missed how disappointed they must be? It was something they had saved up for for so long. And because of her bills, everything had been pushed back.

She leaned her forehead against the cupboard door.

This was how she had felt when Adrian had died.

Useless, incompetent, of no good to anyone.

And now, she had bigger responsibilities and yet was worse off.

Tears scratched at her throat. "I don't know what to do. I've been trying so hard to keep everything together. I just…"

"So make it easier on yourself and them. Let me help. You've handled everything single-handedly all this while. But you don't need to anymore.

"Isn't that why you set this whole thing in motion?"

"So you want me to take your handouts and be happy about it?"

"No, I want you to get the rest you deserve so that Izzie doesn't worry about you."

"You should've talked to me first before you campaigned my parents to your side. How about if you ask instead of deciding we're coming with you?"

Autocratic wasn't enough to describe the man's attitude.

"Is this a war of wills then, Alexis? I'm proposing this so that Isabella can spend time with my family and you can recover easier, too. It won't be long before the stress you're under translates to Isabella. I could not leave everything here as is, knowing the situation."

"Stop speaking as if her very life is unstable," she protested, a lump in her throat. That sense of failure was a lead weight in her chest.

"Not unstable, no. But it is clear that the accident has made everything harder."

Which was exactly the conclusion she had come to. Yet hearing it from his mouth scraped her pride.

Of all the things, what was this compulsion to prove herself to him? Why did his opinion matter this much? Why did his concern, which she was slowly realizing was a huge part of what made Leandro, feel so personal?

"What about your wedding?"

His gaze instantly shuttered. "What about it?"

"Luca told me that your fiancée's father is pushing for a summer wedding."

If she didn't have absolute belief in his prized self-control, Alex would have thought he was close to violence. Such fury blazed in his eyes at the mention of Luca. "You have been talking to Luca?"

"He called to say hello to Izzie and yes, we chatted, a couple of times. I don't think us being there before your wedding is a good idea. The last thing I want is for your new bride or her family to treat Izzie like I was treated."

"They won't."

"What about me?"

When had he swallowed up the distance she'd put between them? Her heart raced as he gently pushed a lock of hair behind her ear. "No one will hurt you, *cara*."

"I can see the headlines now." She kept her tone casual through sheer effort, loath to betray how the idea of his wedding haunted her. The thought of him with his new bride, those hands of his caressing some unknown figure, of laying those lips on another woman, of that inscrutable gray gaze widening with desire…her lack of sleep had gotten worse since she'd seen him again.

He'd laid every concern of hers to rest and yet made her restless to her very bones.

"Leandro Conti's Love Child's Trashy Single Mom a Distinguished Guest at His Wedding to an Heiress…"

A smile broke through the austerity of his face, transforming his face into breathtaking beauty. Even white teeth flashed at her, one edge of his mouth turning up crooked.

Breath catching in her throat, Alex swallowed hard. "Reading Italian tabloids?"

Heat poured through her cheeks. She had given in and scoured for news on him. The lurid headlines and gossip that seemed to always swirl around his family explained Antonio's vulgar words to her. But what had amazed her was Leandro's lack of the same.

And she'd faced the hard truth—that he had trusted her without proof. Even before he'd seen Izzie's pictures.

That he was honorable made it so much harder for her to hate him.

"I assure you I will protect you, Alexis."

"Thanks but no thanks. I saw how you sprang to my defense when Antonio was—"

"I was in shock and you shut him up promptly. Like no one has ever done. No one will say a word to you, I promise you that."

"How can you guarantee that? There'll probably be a million guests at your wedding and they'll surely wonder who I am and I can't stand to be the object of such gossip. Not to mention being a fourth wheel between your new bride and you and your family and her family and—"

One tapered finger landed on her mouth, burning the soft flesh of her lower lip. "Will you send Izzie by herself with me then?"

She swatted his hand away. "No! I...she's a baby, Leandro and a week doesn't make you anything less than a stranger."

Her answer seemed to please him. "Then what I suggest is the only solution we have. I would like to spend time with Isabella."

"But I—"

"*Dio*, Alexis!" Impatience made his tone staccato, harsh. "No one will say anything because there will not be a wedding."

CHAPTER SIX

THERE WASN'T GOING to be a wedding.

Alex couldn't understand how the small, brusquely delivered fact could have such hold over her, even after four days.

Four days in which, somehow, she had let Leandro and her family persuade her that spending the summer with the Contis at their Lake Como villa was a good idea all around.

No sooner than she, only in possession of half her faculties, had admitted that Izzie would love to see more of him than Leandro had seen to and settled a hundred things that needed to be done.

A new manager had been hired for as long as was needed for the store. Her parents had been dispatched on a holiday to Australia as they had initially planned before Alex's accident, with no necessity overlooked. The traitors they were, they'd been more than happy to be on their way and more importantly, out of Leandro's way.

All of her insurance matters had been assigned to a lawyer hired by Leandro for the express purpose of seeing to them. Even the mortgage on her parents' house had been refinanced and the monthly payments taken care of, aided in no small financial way by him. And her and Isabella's visas to Italy taken care of with an expediency that reeked not only of the Contis' wealth but the sheer reach of their power.

It had left Alex gasping for breath one afternoon, wondering what she had invited into her life.

Tucked away in Izzie's bedroom under the guise of packing, she had buried her head between her knees. Sought escape from the feeling of her life being taken over.

Leandro had gone far and beyond anything she'd expected of him when she'd gone to him for reassurance that Izzie would be taken care of. And yet, a small thread of anxiety persisted at the speed with which he'd had their trip arranged.

Apparently, when Leandro had decided that he was very much interested in spending the summer with his daughter, he had meant it quite seriously.

If only she could get a firm grasp on herself and her reaction to his broken engagement... But he had told her nothing about his reason.

That marriage will not suit me anymore, he'd told her with a chillingly heartless calculation. Engulfed by a barrage of unwanted emotions that had hit her, she hadn't asked him any of the questions that pestered her.

For all that her worries about Izzie and her future were calmed, at least temporarily, she still wasn't sleeping well. Much as she had fought it for four days, the crux of it haunted her thoughts.

That Leandro was unattached was what made her anxious, and restless and a thousand other things she was ashamed to admit, even to herself.

It was as if a dam that held all her less than right thoughts at bay was suddenly broken and every insidiously hungry thought and desire was free to roam now.

He was everything that had attracted her back then, a thousand times more now.

Now she knew he was also honorable, that a warmth filled his gaze when he spoke of his wife, that even as he had discarded her the next morning, it had been driven by that sense of betrayal, that family and responsibility and duty were important to him.

Even as it grated, the ease and efficiency with which he'd taken over everything, it was hard not to bask in that. Hard not to feel pleasure at being looked after like that.

Hard not to take it personally.

She didn't want to want him like this.

She didn't want to fall into this trap of imagining things between them, of falling this low as to feel some kind of relief at knowing that he was unattached now. She deserved better than to want a man who thought of her as a betrayal, who tolerated her presence for the sake of his daughter.

Fortunately for her fragmenting peace of mind, she hadn't been alone with Leandro the past few days at their home. Izzie and her parents had seen to that. And on the flight, when Izzie had fallen asleep, Alex had claimed to be tired, not falsely, and retired to the rear cabin and the inviting bed.

A couple of hours later, when he sat down on the narrow bed next to her, Alex jerked into such stringent awareness that her heart ratcheted in her chest.

The solid length of his legs next to her was alien yet alluringly comforting. Musk and something so intensely Leandro coated her every breath. Slowly, he pulled her hand into his and traced the scars.

There was nothing sexual in the touch, still, it burned through her, shaking loose some strange knot of yearning.

He wasn't a tactile person, she'd noticed. Especially when it came to her, there was something very measured, very contained about his movements.

Unable to bear the tension any longer, she turned and opened her eyes.

The softly fading light in the cabin caressed the aquiline nose, the sweepingly sharp cheekbones. Softened the austere set of his mouth. Heat from his body enveloped her, churning her senses into a frenzy.

"You shouldn't be here," she whispered with not the

least bit of anger she'd wanted in her tone. Instead, she sounded husky, weak. "It's not necessary for you to touch me when Izzie's not around."

Did she imagine the soft glint to his gaze? The reverence in his touch as he traced the veins on her wrist? "I didn't realize I was taking a liberty."

"You expect me to believe you walk around touching women you barely know?" she muttered, her nose tickling against his thigh.

"You don't agree that sharing a daughter affords us a kind of intimacy, *cara*? That it binds us as much as we fight it?"

To be bound to him in any way...just the thought set her shivering.

Warm fingers moved from her hand up her arm, kneaded one shoulder and then rested on her jaw. Moved into her hair and combed through the strands. Alex fisted her hands by her side, every inch of her vibrating.

"No," she managed. "Intimacy and friendship and all such rights have to be earned. You and I...strangers who share a daughter. That you slept with me seven years ago doesn't entitle you to anything with me now."

Suddenly, his grip tightened in her hair. Not hurting but just enough to make her scalp tingle with awareness. The rough movement forced her chin up to face him. Something feral bared in his gaze, tearing at the mask of polite civility that embodied Leandro. "Such foul language from such a beautiful mouth, *cara*?"

But it was gone as fast as it came, just as his grip gentled immediately. She didn't know what to make of that momentary fracture in his facade. "It's exactly what you said."

"As far as rights are concerned," the honeyed warmth of his tone didn't hide the steel beneath, "your well-being directly affects my daughter. That means I can interfere if I think you need help.

"You lied to me. You said you were sleeping better but I heard you. I do not like that fear, that anxiety in your tone."

Her cheek tingled where his knuckles rested. Hadn't she just told him off?

"Pity then, isn't it?" She scooted on the soft cotton to get away from him and ended up even closer to the solid muscle of his thigh. "That you can't order the panic gone, that you can't order out that stress for me in that imperious way of yours."

Now, he traced the bridge of her nose, hovered over her mouth. Her pulse raced. Lungs burned.

"You sound angry, Alexis. I have never met a woman who didn't appreciate the benefits that come with my name and wealth. Will you resent me just for solving your problems? Will you resent me because I'm more interested in Isabella than you wanted?

"Or is it that you're still attracted to me?"

"Don't...presume things about me."

"I'm not presuming your racing pulse." His thumb landed at the incriminating spot on her neck. "Or hitching breath or the fact that you're tense like a bow." Long fingers stroked over the nooks and crevices of her shoulders, back and forth until she felt as though there was steel infused in her very veins. "Or that you jump like a cat every time I come near you."

"Being attracted to you doesn't mean I'm willing. I won't be a convenient itch for you to scratch while you play at being daddy for the summer. Like I was some compensation prize after your broken engagement."

"Playing at daddy?" A thread of anger spewed in his question.

"Isn't that what you're doing?"

"I assure you no, Alexis. I intend to take care of Isabella. I intend to be a proper father. If not for me, Luca and

Tina would have suffered neglect. I don't know if I made a difference even. And I will not let that be Izzie's fate."

"She's not neglected."

"But a father is important, *si*?

"Not just for the summer either. The sooner you accept that the better. I'm not grief-stricken over my broken engagement, *cara*.

"Marriage to Sophia was a business alliance. Breaking it had consequences that I'm now prepared to handle. Family comes before business, before anything else for me."

The steely resolve in his tone sent her heart thudding against her rib cage.

He wanted to be a proper father to Izzie?

Had seeing Izzie, who was truly a mirror image of him, triggered some dormant fatherly instinct and decided the matter for him?

Hadn't she read somewhere that nature made children in the image of their fathers so that they bonded with them?

Would he feel differently once he realized how hard being a parent was? How life changed because of a little girl?

"And when you marry eventually? Can you give me the reassurance that your new wife will not resent Izzie? Can you reassure me that you won't resent her for all the changes she'll bring to your life?

"I didn't give up my social life because I like being a martyr.

"I gave it up because none of the men I met would have loved Izzie like a father should. Only Justin—"

"Look at me, Alexis." His grip turned steely against her jaw, forcing her to look at him. The muscle in his jaw jumped. Gray eyes held a stormy anger. Banked, yes, but the fire showed a Leandro she didn't recognize. "My daughter already has a father. *Me*. I will not let any man take that away from me. No other man can take that place in your life."

"You've no right to tell me that I can't have another man in my life, Leandro."

"You just told me you've never met a man who would love Izzie like his own." Frustration made his tone rise, but he wrested himself under control immediately. "We both want the same thing for Isabella. And for what we want, there are not many options left to us."

Shock coursing through every vein, Alex stared at him numbly.

What the hell did he mean by that? Did he want her to move to Italy? Was he suggesting that they live together just for Izzie's sake? Or was he—

God, no! The other alternative was outrageous to even think about.

Suddenly, all Alexis wanted was to be back in her parents' tiny house with her never-ending financial problems and the store and even her fault-finding mother.

Anywhere but here, on this luxurious flight, with this man who'd taken over her life.

That same sensation of careening out of control came at her with a vicious force. "Either you're crazy or I am, because I don't think you suggested what I think you did."

He shrugged. "With Isabella's future in mind, we will come to an agreement that suits us both."

An agreement that suited them both...

"After we land, I will be gone for a week. Will you be all right at the villa? Antonio will be around."

The thought of a reprieve from Leandro and his outrageous ideas made her shudder in relief. She could deal with a hundred Antonios better than her own weakness for this man. "Yes. Of course. I understand that you have your life and commitments."

"Being here has caused too many bottlenecks in the

company, made me realize I need to delegate more. After Rosa's death, I threw myself into work. But I don't want Izzie to feel like I'm neglecting her any longer."

"Leandro?"

"Yes, Alexis?"

"You said Rosa always wanted children and couldn't conceive."

His entire, polite demeanor faded at the mere mention of his wife's name. "Yes?"

"What about you? Did you want to be a father?"

Silence had never been so fraught or so distorted for it felt like an age to Alexis before he answered.

Her stomach twisted into a knot as if her very fate depended on his answer.

"*Si.* I was ready to be a father."

Before she could absorb that, he reached for her.

Cradled her jaw with one hand and pressed his mouth to the corner of hers. Insidious heat unfurled through every nerve. Her fingers dug into his arms, toes curled as she fought the hardest battle of her life.

To not shift and cover his mouth completely. To not throw herself headlong into the need vying for life.

Lips soft and hard at once moved against her tingling skin, sending arrows of pleasure directly to the center of her sex. "You, Alexis, *are* no consolation prize or a cheap summer fling."

This time, when his hands moved over her shoulders and down her trembling body, over her waist, and hips and back up again, long fingers grazing the sides of her breasts, there was no gentleness. No comforting or soothing.

No gentling or caring.

But bold and roving and hungrily masculine and demandingly insistent. Those large hands of his touched desperately but not enough, luring her with a promise of more with his rough strokes. An exploration of the fire that burned between them the moment they touched each other.

That sinuous mouth moved an inch and an inch over, until he covered her own completely.

Such pleasure filled her that Alex groaned loudly. The sound vibrated through her bringing a threadbare rope of caution back.

"You think I would welcome advances from you two minutes after your engagement is broken? You think I'm so eager to fall back into that pattern again?"

It was every shameful thought she'd indulged in herself, and yet, she drew strength from the fact that she called him on it.

But he didn't even budge an inch. Instead, he took over the space between them. Until their legs tangled. Until her breasts grazed his chest. Until even the thought of Izzie softly snoring on the bed in the front was driven from her head.

Only he and his stroking hands and strangely intense gaze remained. Only her awareness of him remained. Only this strange intimacy that she had denied him and yet he claimed remained.

How many times had she dreamed of a moment like this over the past seven years?

One hand under her chin, he tilted it up to face him. "In seven years, I have tried, *so hard*, to forget that night. To pretend like it never happened, *si*. But I never thought such a cheap thing of you." His sigh rattled loudly in the cabin.

The reluctance in his tone made his statement all the more powerful. Made her insides into a pool of molten craving.

"I want you, *cara*. Just as I did all those years ago," he muttered it as if it was a curse. As if he had accepted defeat. "Since the moment you walked into that lounge, guns blazing."

Feral satisfaction filled every nerve, every cell.

To hear him admit that he wanted her, despite his discipline and control, a wildness, a raw sense of power filled her. She gave in to the sheer freedom of it. Just a stolen second, she told herself, before she became a mother and a daughter and a hundred other roles again.

Tremors took hold of her entire body as he continued trailing that mouth all over her face. Nose, brow, jaw, chin—it was as if he opened little portals of pleasure.

It was as if his touch could say things he couldn't. And in sensually overwhelming contrast, his big body shuddered as he took her mouth again.

Alex felt her pulse vibrate everywhere—in her neck, her heavy breasts, her shaking knees and in the wet place between her thighs.

With his hot mouth devouring hers, Leandro slammed her against himself.

Alex climbed over him like a vine, the jut of his erection a hot press against her belly. She arched against him, looped her leg around his until she was riding his thigh.

Leandro egged her on, his fingers crawling under her silk blouse. The slap of his abrasive palm against her heated flesh, the slow exploration up her skin, her nipples distended against her cotton bra, desperate for his touch.

Alex moaned, and moved over him, mindless in her pursuit of pleasure. It was when his fingers reached the seam of her bra and pushed inside that Alex realized what she was allowing.

God, she had acted just as she said she wouldn't.

A frustrated cry fell from her lips but he didn't release her.

His forehead touched hers, his breath feathered her. Lips stinging from the raw assault of his, shame permeating her, she closed her eyes.

"Do you not see the inevitability of this, Alexis? Of

how right everything is this time between us? How easily you melt in my hands, how I could make you scream with the slightest of touches? All the intimacies you'll give, all your desires, all your needs, your every breath will be mine again.

"You will be mine."

Such arrogance reverberated in his voice should have made her furious. And yet…at the core of her, she trembled at the want in it, at the intensity in it.

No one had ever wanted her like that. No one had ever put it into words like that.

With that reply, he left without glancing at her again.

Knees shaking, her sex aching for a release that wasn't coming, Alex slid to the bed. He had everything so perfectly mapped out without even telling her.

Had he truly just switched the candidate for his wife from one woman to her? Was he that heartless? Did Leandro want a future with her, just for Izzie's sake?

And if he did, *Dear God*, what was she going to do?

CHAPTER SEVEN

IN THE PROCESS of undoing his cuffs, Leandro stilled. Sounds of splashing waves accompanied by Izzie's giggles, Luca's deep laughter, Valentina's broken English and Alexis's husky warnings…it was pure cacophony at the villa. Like he'd never heard.

The afternoon sun beating down on him, he took the steps to the veranda like an eager schoolboy.

It seemed as if the entire villa was awash in a burst of sound and activity, unlike it had ever seen.

A small bicycle with training wheels and pink streamers lay against the marble pillar. An English paperback and a pink iPod lay on the bench in the garden.

Something in him flinched at the alien sounds and sights. At the sudden absence of that dark, deep silence that he'd become used to for so long.

Only now did he realize how much the silence of the past two decades had become a part of the tall pillars, the marble floors and even their very psyches. He'd thought he had made the villa a home for all three of them. But suddenly he wasn't so sure for he had never heard such joy in the air.

The scent of jasmine felt richer, the sky felt bluer, the entire world felt as if it had transitioned from a gray, bleary morning to spring sunshine.

He closed his eyes and let his hearing amplify, let the sounds wash over him. He didn't feel peaceful as he had during his marriage with Rosa, but then he didn't expect life with Izzie to be peaceful.

He'd already accepted that life with Alexis wasn't going to be peaceful.

And yet, strangely the thought excited him more than it made him uneasy.

It had taken him a week to wrap up the most urgent of his business obligations and return to their villa. He had spoken to Izzie a few times since then but every time, Alex refused to say anything except that they were doing okay.

Had he pushed her too far too soon?

He hadn't meant to confront her like that on the flight, he hadn't meant to touch her so intimately while their daughter lay asleep so close, but again, Alexis had fragmented his careful planning.

Running a hand through his hair, he strolled out into the veranda and looked at the pool. With the background of the gleaming blue of the pool, his gaze instantly found her.

Clad in a modestly cut, pink bikini, her blond hair framing her face in damp waves, Alexis sat above with her pink toes skimming the water. A serene smile touched her features as she closed her eyes and raised her face to the sun. Luca and Tina were playing with Izzie in the pool.

Two seconds, that's all he could manage before his gaze turned back to her again.

Lush and lithe, her scantily clad body was a siren's lure. He felt as if he'd been handed a treasure and didn't know where to start or what to look at.

He devoured the dips and valleys of her breasts and waist and hips, the honeyed sheen to her skin, the thick swathes of her hair like a starving man. Or a youth who was looking at a woman's body for the first time.

His hands itched to hold those lush breasts, trace that concave plane of her stomach. He would kiss and lick and taste every inch of that silky flesh. Those long legs would wrap around him as he pushed into her...

Would she scream his name like she had done seven

years ago? Would that sheer, abandoned pleasure of it send him careening toward his own release?

Dio, he hadn't gotten hard like this at the mere sight of a woman even in puberty.

As if she could sense his lustful thoughts, her elegant neck turned this way and that. And then she looked up.

Their gazes held and clashed over the distance, a pink flush suddenly seeping up her neck and cheeks. He saw the stiffness that descended in her shoulders, the vulnerability in her mouth that in turn made her spine straighten as she realized the intentions he didn't hide in his eyes.

She read him as clearly as if he had told her what he intended to do to her and with her.

Her brown gaze widened, her palm moved over her neck in a betraying gesture and then her mouth pursed. That same gaze now flashed fire at him.

With his heart pounding, he watched as she stood up in a smooth movement, like a gazelle rising from a pond. Challenge simmered in every line of her body as she walked to the lounger, picked up a tube of sun lotion and went back the pool.

Tension a live beast roaring inside him, he waited. Instantly, he realized what she was going to do. He knew she was only doing it to provoke him, to challenge him. To drive him mad. To tell him she wasn't going to fall in line so easily.

But it didn't help quiet the acrid burn in his gut.

The husky tone of her voice reached him, a mild thread outside the roaring in his ears. On cue, Luca climbed out of the pool, said something that made her laugh and put his hands on her shoulders.

Covering her breasts with her crossed hands, Alexis turned and gave Luca her back. Hands full of sunscreen, Luca undid the thin string of her bikini top, pushed it out of his way and slathered it all over her skin.

A burst of violent emotion claimed him as he looked at them transfixed.

Those elegant, artistic hands of his brother's roamed freely over the woman that belonged to him.

Skin and sinew that Leandro wanted to touch, curves that Leandro wanted to claim, laughter that he wanted to evoke…all in Luca's hands.

Sweat beaded his brow, his entire body a taut mass of frustrated desire and rampaging fury.

He had warned Luca to stay away. Of course, his brother wouldn't listen. He knew in a rational part of his mind that Luca didn't even want her. That he would not take what was Leandro's. But he would cross any line just to rile Leandro, just to push him out of his comfort zone.

Lines that neither of them could come back from…

"She pits your brother against you." Antonio's fractured English broke the grip of his anger. "I did not like that woman seven years ago and I do not trust her now. Keep your child and get rid of her."

Leandro cringed at the reckless order. "I couldn't have asked for a better mother for Isabella." Even as he committed another betrayal toward Rosa, Leandro knew it was the truth.

Rosa had been brought up traditionally, had leaned on him for strength, had been obedient, caring. If they had had children, he knew she would have bowed to Antonio's will in their upbringing.

It would have been Leandro's battle to fight.

But Alexis was like a fierce lioness.

Even as she fought her own insecurities, Alexis didn't back down, not once when it came to Isabella. "I will not separate them and fracture my family as Enzo did. She belongs with me, just as Izzie does."

"I did not think I would see the day when you would let a woman weaken you."

Dio, the last thing he wanted was to discuss Alexis with his grandfather. "You have no idea what you're talking about."

"Are you so blinded by lust that you can't see that she's manipulating you? You think she doesn't know that you stand here like a lust-crazed fool watching your shameless brother flirt with her, put his hands on her?"

A grim smile broke Leandro's mouth. Lust-crazed he might be but he was no fool. He had been right.

Alexis wasn't one to meekly fall into his plans. That he had brought her this far was only due to her insecurities and because he was ruthless when he set his mind to something. Despite her grief about her brother, despite thinking of herself as second-rate with her parents, she'd done everything for them.

The challenge of conquering her, of bending her to his will, of making her his own sizzled in his blood now. "I do not like what she just did any more than you do, but I know why she did it."

When he was through with her, she was going to wish she hadn't started it. No, scratch that.

She was going to like everything he was going to do to her. He was going to indulge himself and her, until the thought of even challenging him and his rights with her was driven from her mind.

A derisive glint entered Antonio's eyes. "I've never seen you look at a woman like that. Not even poor Rosa. This woman is not good for you. It is obvious she's after our name."

Masking the anger that filled him so easily, *so uncharacteristically*, for his grandfather had always been a man of crude words, Leandro filled his tone with cutting ice. "Rosa and Alexis are different kinds of women. Once Alexis realizes this is for the best, once she understands what I want from this marriage, it will work just fine.

"But do not speak of her in that tone, Nonno. I will not tolerate it again."

"You would go against me for a woman who slept with you after—"

Raising his hand, Leandro cut Antonio off. Let the old man see his ire. "She will be my wife. She is the mother of my child. She is your best chance at a future Conti male heir that you're so desperate for. I suggest you afford her the respect she deserves.

"Enzo let you browbeat Mamma, but I will not allow it. Whatever our private arguments, Alexis is not to hear even one of your complaints. Not if you want to see your great-grandchildren."

Chin lifting in mutiny, his grandfather glared at him. "What about the trouble Salvatore will cause with the board? He will not take kindly to you breaking your engagement to Sophia."

"Kairos Constantinou."

"That reckless Greek magnate? That's your answer?" The combined awe and horror in Antonio's voice only confirmed Leandro's decision. The Conti board needed new blood. He was tired of being the only one who had to steer it in new directions since Luca even refused to be on the board. "You thought his investment strategies were too bold in this financial climate," Antonio continued.

"Yes but Kairos proved me wrong. An alliance between us will work well." He waited for Antonio to digest it.

Kairos had grown up on the streets of Athens, built a powerful export empire, was hungry for alliances in the Old World that still looked at him and shunned him because of his background. Leandro had exactly what Kairos wanted—the Conti name that went back hundreds of years—and Kairos had what he wanted.

For all his reckless investments and hunger for power,

there was an integrity to Kairos that Leandro liked, a strength that he needed.

Already Kairos had arrived in Italy and started working on his piece of their alliance.

The threat from Salvatore was taken care of. Valentina's future was set. If only he could settle Luca's future, too. Once his alliance with Kairos was solidified, he'd have to think of it.

All that was left was for him to marry Alexis. His world would be back on its track.

"You trained me well, Nonno. Now, trust me to handle the company and the family."

After several more minutes, finally, Antonio relented. "I do trust you, Leandro. Neither will I stop protecting you and even Luca." That he left out Valentina scraped Leandro raw but that was a battle he'd learned long ago to not fight.

No matter, because soon Valentina wouldn't care that she didn't have Conti blood in her veins.

But his grandfather was nowhere near done. "Did you know this woman you trust so implicitly has been speaking with a travel agent? That she purchased two tickets back to New York in a couple of weeks? Exactly the week during which you are scheduled to travel to the Middle East on business?"

"You're playing a treacherous game, *bella*," Luca whispered in her ear as he tied back the strings of her bikini top with an efficiency that spoke volumes. "I didn't think you were the manipulative kind, playing my brother against me."

Alex cringed. Shame made her voice thin. "I'll be sad to lose you as a friend but I did what I had to do, Luca. I have to somehow fight your brother's arrogant assumptions."

"And is it so important to fight Leandro, Alex?"

"Someone has to make him learn he can't control everything." Even now, she couldn't believe the arrogance of his words, her own weakness that she hadn't even mustered a reply. "Someone needs to cut him down to size."

His laughter instantly soothed Alex's shame. She turned and as always, the words on her mouth faltered at the masculine perfection of Luca's features.

No man should have such beauty, such perfection that everything was handed over to him on a platter. That the whole world crumbled to its knees for that smile. That no woman would look past it to the man beneath, she suddenly realized.

Yet, she had always preferred Leandro's austere, almost stark beauty to Luca's overwhelming perfection.

Unlike the forbidding man whose face had become hauntingly tight at what she had done, Luca was always touching her. He did so now, framing her face with his hand.

Wicked humor shone in his jet-black eyes. "Are they still standing there?"

Alex peeked out of the corner of her vision. The dark specter of Leandro and Antonio standing over them turned her tummy into jelly. "Yes, but Luca, I'm not interested in you," she added hurriedly.

"You wound me, Alex." Pure laughter filled his words and she exhaled roughly. "What is it that my brother possesses that I don't?"

"Less cockiness in his own beauty, like a peacock, for starters," she said, raising a brow. Laughter carved dimples in his cheeks. "Not that I'm interested in Leandro either."

A sober light filled his gaze. "Resistance is futile if he's decided that he's interested, *cara*. And having seen the fury in his eyes just now, I don't think it is in question anymore."

Alarm made her question sharp. "Is that a threat to fall in line with his wishes?"

"No, *bella*." He brought her hand to his lips and kissed it. "Just a warning from a friend. I'm sure Antonio has already informed him that you bought tickets for you and Izzie to New York. I can't let him have all the odds."

Alex stepped back from him, aghast that he knew. She had made herself crazed with anxiety, cleaved herself in two before she'd decided to buy them. But just like earlier, she needed something to calm her agitation, she needed an exit strategy whether she used them or not.

"How do you know? Damn it, how does Antonio know?"

Luca shrugged. "Doesn't matter. What matters is that you've declared war on my brother by flirting with me. By buying those tickets."

"He started it. I just armed myself."

"No one's ever called me a weapon before." He preened and pouted. "I'm not sure whether to be amused or insulted."

His mock hurt expression sent her to giggles just as it did Izzie.

"Your laughter is music, *bella*, your spirit so pure," he said a wistful note to it. The jet-black of his gaze warmed for an infinitesimal moment, showing a glimpse of desperation that caught Alex's breath. "Maybe you'll prefer me instead of Leandro?"

A stinging retort rose to her lips but Alex held it back. She didn't mistake that he was attracted to her.

No, what Luca liked was the idea of what she represented to Leandro.

Shock widened her eyes as she caught a facet of the playboy that no one probably ever saw. She smiled and kissed his cheek, immensely glad to call him a friend. "Now, I know why they call you the Conti Devil."

He offered his arm and Alex linked hers around it. They started a slow walk around the exquisitely manicured lawn.

Lush greenery dotted with Japanese trees and bouquets of bougainvillea. But through every step, and every breath, Alex was aware of the presence of Leandro behind her.

She couldn't help but notice Luca carefully kept them in view of the terrace.

"That I can make you laugh is going to drive him crazy the most."

"You think so?"

"Yes, we used to compete to try to make Valentina laugh. But Leandro, you see, never had a chance to be a carefree child, to play pranks. It drove him nuts that I always won with Tina. She was this tiny, skinny thing and took ages to trust us, to get used to us. Although, it's him she goes to when she's upset, she comes to me for laughs."

Alex frowned. "Used to you?"

Luca's carefree mouth tightened and it changed the entire vista of his face. "Valentina lived with our mother until she died. When we heard of her death, Leandro brought her to live with us. It was the first time we met each other. Until then, we did not know that we had a sister."

"Leandro brought her here, not Antonio?"

"No. Antonio had his reservations about Tina. But from the moment we learned about her, Leandro wouldn't rest."

Family means everything to me, he'd said on the flight.

"How old was he?"

"Fifteen."

With every word Luca uttered, Alex's panic mounted. It felt as though something was rushing at her at breakneck speed and she was stuck in its way. Just like the truck that had crashed into her sedan. Except this time, it was her heart that could get crushed into tiny little pieces.

One kiss…she'd shared one kiss with the man and somehow her heart had already taken a beating? How had she left herself so vulnerable to his manipulations? How did she extricate herself without harming Izzie?

"Only fifteen?" she mumbled, hoping Luca would keep talking. Even as she knew that he was manipulating her in his own way.

"*Si.* Even then Leandro was set in his ways. He argued with Antonio for days, relentless in his belief that Tina belonged with us, that she have a home with us." His jet-black gaze held hers. He took Alex's hands in his and squeezed. The comfort he offered made her spine tingle with warning. "My brother will do anything to protect those he considers his, Alex. Whatever he has done or will do, he wants the best for Izzie. And you."

"But I'm not his," she whispered back. "He can't have me because he's decided it should be so."

Suddenly, Alexis understood everything she hadn't seen until now. Chills broke out on her bare skin even as the sun warmed her.

Leandro had never intended to be a stranger to Izzie. Even before they had left, he'd known that. He had accompanied her to New York knowing that he was going to bring them back here.

He'd told her nothing, let her believe that it was a burden she'd brought on him. Let her wrangle around in her own confusion and fears.

The fury in his eyes when Justin had asked Izzie when she would return, the stony gaze when Alex had mentioned bringing another man into her and Izzie's life, everything made sense now.

Chest tight, throat raw, Alex wanted to hit something.

Fingers cold on her skin, Luca stroked her shoulders, as if to calm her. As if he understood how close to the surface her temper was. "Should I tell you what else I think he's saying to Antonio, Alex?"

Forehead resting on his shoulder, for Alex felt as weak with emotion as a leaf that could be swayed by the wind, she nodded.

"I'm sure he warned Antonio to never disrespect you again. That he will banish him from his life if he ever hears him say so."

Tears knocked at her eyelids and Alex held them at bay with her last thread of will. "You've no idea what you're asking me to overlook just because he means well."

Her insecurity with her parents.

Her weakness after the accident.

Her fear that she might fail Izzie too…as she'd failed at everything else.

Leandro had learned all her fears and insecurities, while she had thought him genuinely caring, and he'd taken each one and used it all against her.

He'd caged her with good intentions and her own need to do the right thing by everyone around her.

"I know what my brother could do in his drive to do his duty. Just give him a chance, Alex. See if he's worthy of you. Do not let pride stand in your way. If you find not, I'll personally help you in your fight against him."

"And will there be a fight, Luca?"

"If you take Izzie and walk away from him? If you deprive Izzie of her own father because Leandro has his own way of doing things, because he's the most arrogant, domineering brute in the whole world?" Luca's laugh was harsh, filled with his own complaints against his brother. "Yes, *bella*." He sounded full of regret at the very prospect. "It would be a sad day if two of the most deserving people I know start tearing into each other with a child in between."

With Luca's dire-sounding prospect still ringing in her ears, Alex returned to her suite. Mind churning, she helped Izzie bathe and then picked at some fruit and olives and sipped her cold white wine. Restless to her very bones, she weaved a path through the lakefront sitting room that her suite afforded.

The vista stole her breath as it did every morning.

Luminous and blue with boats drifting lazily up and down, tiny villages glinting in the sunlight, it was a far cry from her life in Brooklyn.

But with Leandro manipulating and directing their relationship whichever way he wanted, using her own weakness against her, Alex knew the same vista, the same idyllic villa could become a gilded cage. Could choke her spirit even worse than her parents' blueprint for a perfect child had done all these years.

Finally, she called Emma.

Within minutes, she was spewing the whole sorry story into the handset, angry and outraged. And more than anything, she realized, hurt.

Had his desire for her been a pretense, too? A convenient lie to bind herself to his side? She had already betrayed how much that night seven years ago had meant to her, hadn't she? She had told him all about how curtailed her life had been after having Izzie.

The sense of betrayal was deepest in this, as if he'd taken the very thing she had handed him and carved into her.

Forget Leandro's manipulations, do you want him, Alex? Do you think he's worth taking a chance on?

Forget your house, your store, your parents and even Izzie. Think of yourself before you make a decision because this is your life.

Emma's brutally incisive questions were still racking her brain when a maid knocked at her door.

Shell-shocked and confused still, Alex mutely took the two expensive bags with designer labels.

Only when Izzie excitedly opened the bag and a beautiful, silky pink dress slipped out did she remember the party tonight.

An informal get-together of their extended family and closest friends so that they could meet Izzie, Tina had informed her last night. With shaking hands, Alex opened the velvet case.

The clipped sound of the tiny latch unhooking on the case moved through her like lightning blazed through the sky.

A delicately spun choker of diamonds set in white gold and matching earrings nestled on the navy blue velvet bed, glittering brightly in the sunlight that shafted through the windows.

Diamonds for the strongest woman I know, the curly script read.

A tingling began in her chest as she read it over and over again. Even the glittering diamonds paled in contrast to the words that moved through her like thunder and lightning.

If he'd said beautiful or smart, she would have wrote it off as another manipulation.

But calling her strong, the one thing she prided herself on, the one thing she had forced herself to be through Adrian's death and her parents' disappointment and having Izzie and her accident, it was as if he had shot an arrow direct to her heart.

As if he truly understood her.

As if he truly saw her and cherished her.

She'd been an open book to him. There was still every chance that he was manipulating her.

With his handwritten note fluttering in her hand, Alex sat on the cool tiled floor and closed her eyes.

Emma was right. With the accident and the store and Izzie and her parents' continual disappointment in her, she had forgotten something important. With or without Leandro's help, she would never do wrong by Izzie.

She loved her little girl more than anything in life.

The simple acknowledgement freed her to breathe, made her heart lighter.

For the first time in years, Alex focused on herself. On

her wants and desires. That her mind instantly fluttered to Leandro's kiss only made her smile. Her fingers rose to her lips. She could still feel his mouth on her, the insistent demand in it, the growl that had escaped him when she had tangled her tongue with his.

The way his powerful body had shuddered in supplication when she bit his lower lip, the way he had buried his mouth in her neck and whispered in Italian...

There had been no manipulation in the languid strokes of his mouth, in his desperate caresses, in those urgent whispers.

He could dress it up as duty or the right thing for Izzie or a hundred other things, but the fact was that Leandro wanted her desperately. For a man who prided himself on living by his rules and not emotions, by his duty and not desire, it was huge.

And she wanted him, she wanted to explore the heat between them, she wanted to tell him her secrets and learn his.

Was it enough to begin a relationship with?

Attraction to her and unconditional love for Izzie—could she even ask for more as a start?

Decision made, Alexis unwrapped the paper tissue around the pink dress, the whisper of its silky folds a song to her ears. Held it against herself and looked in the full-length mirror.

She would do this. She would have a relationship with Leandro, see where it took them, but it would be on her terms.

She would own her desire for him, and she would make him own that he wanted her in his life. And not for Izzie's sake or duty's sake or honor's sake.

But because he wanted her. She would have what he owed her this time, even if she had to seduce the truth out of him.

Funny that he'd armed her himself with that dress and those diamonds. He'd given her time, security and the belief that she owed it to herself to enjoy her life, even if he'd done to manipulate her.

Plugging her iPod into the speaker system, Alex turned up the volume on a Lady Gaga song and danced around with Izzie, excitement pulsing through her.

Leandro needed to learn that Alex could wrench away his control as surely as he did hers.

That this time around, Alex wouldn't settle for anything less than what she wanted.

CHAPTER EIGHT

LEANDRO MOVED THROUGH the perfectly manicured gardens and among his family and friends like a pale imitation of himself. No, an agitated, less-than-together version of himself.

The same scent of hydrangeas and jasmine that had calmed him so many times, the stone and marble villa that he had somehow wrested into a home for him, Luca and Valentina now mocked him and his very image of himself.

The disgusting and disconcerting fact was that he had rushed to her bedroom two seconds after Antonio's self-satisfied whisper about her plans. Anger and disbelief and a rope of unease had held him in its grip as he raised his hand and clutched the gleaming chrome door handle.

In a flicker of a moment, from one breath to the next, he had realized what he had been about to do.

Izzie's laughter from within the suite mocked him, scraped him.

He'd been exactly like Enzo had been so many times in one of his violent tempers.

He wouldn't have hit Alex like Enzo had done with his *mamma* that one time or spewed vitriol or called her horrible names. He knew that much. Yet that he had become so angry, so unknowing of where he was going or what he was about to do...so afraid of losing something he hadn't realized he needed.

But Leandro had never needed anything or anyone. His success with the company and being a responsible guard-

ian to his brother and sister, they had all been driven by
the needs of others.

The reminder of his father had been like a naked dip
in the freezing lake that Luca had challenged him to in
one of those rare moments of childhood they had enjoyed.

How had Alexis gotten under his skin? What was it
about her that made him react with such violence of emotion? Why this hunger to claim her as his?

Until now, he had avoided the crowd, needing to cool
his temper before he saw her. Or his brother who'd worn
a smirking grin all evening as they met several of their
cousins and aunts.

It was only years of meticulous habit that he now noticed the uniformed waiters and flowing champagne and
Conti family members that came crawling out to see Isabella. And Alexis, of course, just like she had expected.

Because they all wanted to see the woman that had
made him fall from his pedestal. They expected a stunning
woman armed to the teeth with wiles and cunning. They
would form a line to see his weakness, his...

But something inside him balked at calling her a weakness anymore.

With her simplicity and straightforwardness, Alexis
would be a shock to all of them. She'd probably dress in a
garish tank top and shorts just to insult him and his family.

He had no doubt that she would shred that dress into
pieces, throw that diamond choker he'd selected himself
in the rubbish bin.

"Papà...you're back." He heard Isabella's squeal behind
him.

His mouth instantly curving, he turned and saw her on
the marble steps. Reaching her, he picked her up while she
vined those chubby arms around his neck and held him
tight. Kissed him soundly on his cheek. He stayed there,
suddenly realizing how much he had missed Isabella's in-

cessant chatter in the past week. The sweet scent of her made his throat close up as it always did.

Dio, he had come so close to not knowing her...

"Did you miss me, *piccola*?"

She considered the question and he laughed again. "I had so much fun with Uncle Luca and *Zia* so not a lot, Papà." As if to mollify him, she bent closer and whispered, "You wanna know a secret?"

"*Si.* Your uncle and aunt always hide the best ones from me."

"I peeked at Mamma's special folder yesterday when she was showering."

"Mamma's special folder?" he repeated, some sleek black diary with lots of phone numbers of men she knew instantly coming to mind.

When had he become so inventively distrustful? When had every small facet of Alexis's life become this important to him?

All their lives, Antonio had in turn hated and loved Luca because he was the image of their father.

Right down to his creative pursuits and genius thinking and his looks.

Because he, like Enzo had done at a horrible price to all of them, lived so recklessly and without a direction. That he partied and drank and chased women indiscriminately.

But Luca, as far as Leandro knew, never lost it like he had this afternoon.

Luca, for all he slept with every willing woman, would never touch one in anger or distress.

Suddenly, it felt as if Leandro was the one who had inherited all of his father's disgusting traits—distrust, this sudden temper, this unease as if he was losing control of himself.

The very thought made him cold to his bones. Made him want to ship Alexis back to New York on the next flight before she revealed sides of him he didn't want to face.

"She has a big shelf full of those binders but she brang only—"

"Brought," he corrected as he had seen Alexis do.

"Brought only a few here. She used to draw and write a lot in them before the accident. Now she just opens them and looks at them." Sadness tinged those gray eyes of hers that were so much like his own. "Last week she thought I was sleeping. But I wasn't and I think…she cried when she opened them."

Alexis had been crying?

The image twisted his gut.

Izzie hugged him tighter and he knew the thought of Alexis's tears scared her. "Papà will take care of Mamma, Izzie. She'll never cry again, *si*?"

"*Si*," she replied, her smile wide, her eyes full of pride.

"These folders, what do they have in them, *piccola*?" he asked, refusing to feel even a little guilt for using his daughter as his cohort.

If there was something he could do to take away that sadness from Alexis, he had to know.

"Lots of pictures and stories, Papà. Sometimes, she reads them to me. But not much since her car crashed."

"Why not?"

With the attention of a gnat, Izzie tuned out his question. "Did you see these?" she added, raising her legs upward.

"New frock, *bambina*?" he inquired with the utmost affected interest while his gaze moved upward toward Alexis's bedroom.

Anxiety and something else thrummed through his veins.

Isabella sighed that world-weary sigh of hers that made his heart squeeze every time. That made his chest feel too small for the laughter that roared through him. He did so now while she watched him with a bemused glance.

For his precious six-year-old, it seemed he was not only ancient but also completely out of touch with the modern world she lived in. Like how he was supposed to be buying gadgets and not stick-thin dolls for her. She was forever telling him off for not being savvy enough like Luca. Or for not installing some candy jewel game on his mobile phone.

Apparently, Leandro wasn't hip enough for his daughter. Did Alexis think so, too?

Did she wish he could flirt and charm and do all these fun things like Luca did? Did she truly prefer someone fun-loving and adventurous like Luca to him?

Her husky laughter from this afternoon with Luca played along his nerves like some jarring symphony.

Dio mio, what was she reducing him to?

"Of course I had to wear a new frock to meet all my new family," Isabella said with exaggerated patience. "It's my new pumps." She wiggled her toes again. "*Zio* Luca… *designed* Conti pumps, just for me." Pride rang through her voice, as if she understood the centuries-old legacy.

She barely let him glance at the shiny black leather before she started off again. "Although Mamma says I shouldn't expect new toys and games all the time just because you're stinking rich. Does Italian money stink, Papà?" she then asked innocently.

Laughter barreled out of his chest. His entire body shook with the impact of it and he sank to the steps with Izzie in his arms while his extended family and his closest friends stared at him as if he had grown horns.

Luca and Valentina strolled close and stood stunned, their hearts in their eyes, as if they'd never seen him laughing like that.

Had he ever? Had they been deprived of so much despite his best efforts?

While his little girl went on in that incessant way of hers. "She says it'll make me..." She scrunched her face again and by this time, Leandro was choking with laughter and tears. "... Arrogant and domi...dominairing like some people she knows."

Even Luca and Tina had joined his laughter now.

"I asked what that meant and she said I should ask you. She said you'd know best."

Leandro didn't have a memory of ever laughing like this. Of ever feeling this carefree, of this rightness in his world.

Magpie-like, Izzie went on while a sudden hush fell around the crowd that had moved toward the steps.

Leandro pushed to his feet. He put Izzie down when she wiggled.

Alexis stood at the top of the steps, a vision in the dark pink silk.

Whispers buzzed around him while his family took stock of her but she had eyes for only him.

Leandro felt like a charge of electricity had hit him straight from the sky and held him rooted to the ground.

As if he had waited all his life for this moment where he could feast on Alexis.

There was shock and disbelief and, above all, that sense of wonder, as if he'd been given a gift.

What did it mean that she had worn the dress and jewelry he had sent her? Would she ever act as he expected?

But suddenly he realized there was such profound pleasure in the unexpected with Alexis.

Her strawberry blond hair fell in lustrous waves around her shoulders, framing her distinctive features. And the scar she wore so bravely only made her even more beautiful for him.

The diamond choker he had specially commissioned for her glittered around her swan-like neck.

Slinky straps exposed tanned shoulders while the ruched neckline hinted barely at her cleavage. The silky fabric fell to her ankles molding her long legs.

Shoulders squared, hair gleaming bright, she came down the steps. Only then did he see the thigh-length slit. One toned thigh and a shapely calf winked at him.

Like an engulfing wave, want came at him, drenching him from head to toe. Blood pounded. Instinct roared. Muscles thrummed.

Challenge oozed out of every pore on that sensual body of hers. His mouth dried. And he was hard like stone.

If she meant to prance around all evening in the dress and diamonds that he had bought for her, if this was her idea of Look But Don't Touch, her idea of Privileges Revoked, then Leandro had to hand it to her.

She had devised the perfect form of revenge for his sins against her. She had also somehow taken the sails out of his anger, shaken loose the dread in his gut that she would flee one night with Izzie in hand, just because he had manipulated the truth for his purposes.

That he would wake up one day and not find her there, like he hadn't seen his mother one summer morning. That he would lose this thing, too, one of the most joyous things that had come into his life, like everything had gone before.

Because to be a father to Izzie without Alexis as his wife was just not enough anymore. And not just for Izzie's sake.

For all she bought those tickets, Alexis wouldn't flee in the night. She wouldn't leave without a fight, at least. She was not weak or cowardly.

He was no more Enzo than Alexis was his mother.

History would not repeat in his marriage, in this villa again, he told himself.

It was her way of wresting control of the situation, her way of coping when he had all but taken everything familiar away from her.

He understood her. And *Dio*, he really hoped she would understand, soon, why he had done what he had done. Or else, relief for his ever-present erection was never going to come.

Finally, she halted on the last step right in front of him. It brought her face-to-face with him. The subtle scent of her body teased him, the warmth from her body taunted.

Words came and floated away from his lips, inadequate and much too revealing of emotions he didn't understand himself. "Arrogant and domineering, *bella*? If we're going to coach her to take sides, then the war is truly on, Alexis."

She raised a brow while her eyes glittered like precious stones. "Just teaching our daughter some important facts of life, Leandro. You wouldn't want either of us to get used to this lifestyle and expect diamonds and tiaras for every little occasion now, would you? Even you couldn't buy your way out of everything. Not with the number of things I'm going to have to forgive you for."

Our daughter, she had said.

Was she going to accept what he planned for them? Or was she still going to challenge him at every turn?

He touched her then, as inevitable as his next breath. He lifted her hand and pressed his mouth to her wrist. Felt her tremble beneath his lips. Imagined trailing them over every inch of her.

Slowly, with excruciating reluctance, he returned her hand to her side.

"I would say we were even after that display at the pool this afternoon, no?"

He settled his arm around her waist and nudged her forward. She noted his possessive gesture with a raised brow but didn't say anything. "Not even close. And are you so sure it was a display?"

"Yes." He clasped her arm and pulled her to him. "A cheap ploy, too."

A hint of tease turned her voice molten. "This from the master manipulator? The control freak? The man who let me believe his daughter was a burden, a hurdle in the way of his new happiness?"

While each and every one of his guests watched with a kind of twisted fascination, she cradled his jaw and looked up at him.

As if she owned him. As if she had every right to his body and even his thoughts. As if she had shed all those insecurities and fears and become this bold, stunning creature who owned her every desire.

Heart pounding, Leandro stared at her, his hands fisting at his side. His first instinct was to shove her hand and walk away. He'd never been one for public displays of any kind. *Dio*, he hadn't even danced with Rosa in the public, or touched her this way.

He had never wanted to.

"I'm an old-fashioned man, *cara*," he warned her but it didn't carry any real threat. He sounded husky, rough. "I'll always do what I think is right." That was as far an explanation as he was willing to offer.

She traced his jawline, and then smoothed out the frown on his forehead.

Leandro held himself still, somehow. The sensation of surrendering to her touch and her words was alien yet exhilarating. "Then I'll do whatever I have to do to ensure you do not ruin any chance we have of this working. For once, I'm going to be the one in charge, Leandro, the one who'll protect this relationship. Can you handle that?"

Something danced in her eyes and he realized she understood him far better than anyone had ever done. He had done everything he could do to bring her here, to stake his claim and now she was doing the same.

Slowly the thought of denying her faded away, and stinging need rose in its place. Every other part of him waited in anticipation for her bold touch, for her daring strokes.

Cristo, would this woman ever stop surprising him? Was there any version of her that wouldn't torment and tease him?

Could there be so much fun in relinquishing control?

It both thrilled and haunted him—how much he wanted to give up the reins of their relationship to her.

"I've decided to let you make it up to me for everything you didn't tell me. But no more dresses and extravagant gifts, Leandro. You don't want to confirm your grandfather's belief that I'm for sale, do you?"

He didn't know why he couldn't suddenly tell her the truth or why with her, he acted first and then tried to rationalize his behavior to himself. Seven years ago and now. "You were right in that my family and friends here tonight will dissect every tiny detail about you and Isabella. One of them will speak to the press and there will be a furor about the Conti legacy as there is every ten years.

"I knew you wouldn't want to give them anything more to talk about."

"Meaning my usual clothes would give them something to talk about?"

"Si."

Fire flashed in her eyes. And beneath that a deep vulnerability that he would have given anything to heal. This constant battle to protect the core of what made her *her* versus the desire to use it to bind her to him, it was slowly eroding him from within. "So you're ashamed of me then?"

"No. I'm protective of you, Alexis."

She moved her hands over the diamonds, the dress, her left hand slower than the right. "So this was all to make sure there was no cheap talk about me or Izzie?"

"*Si.*"

"And the note? Was that to shore up my armor against all these people, too? To build up my confidence so that I didn't falter here tonight and humiliate you? Should I make sure I don't talk much so that I don't disappoint their image of the great Leandro Conti?"

"*Si.*"

Her head jerked as if he had slapped her, looked away and then met his gaze again with a wounded defiance. Suddenly, he felt like the lowest of low. "*Dear God,* is there anything real about you? Is there a single word or thought that comes from your heart? Do you possess one, Leandro? Or has it turned into a black lump and rotted?"

"No, Alexis." He clasped her arm before she could turn away. "Hear me. I wrote it because I thought you needed to hear it, *si*, that you needed the courage to face this crowd. But, *cara*, I also wrote it because it's the truth.

"Because it's something you should be told again and again."

Something glittered in her gaze then.

She bent toward him so suddenly that his thoughts scattered. His nostrils flared with the subtle scent of her skin and soap. "If you want this thing to work between us, if you want me to give this a chance, I need more, Leandro.

"I need more than duty and Izzie's welfare and family values. I need more than glittering jewels and designer labels and manipulative words.

"Even struggling at everything I tried, I've been a good daughter and a mom. And I always will be. With you or without you. Just Izzie's happiness is not enough for this to work.

"In this thing between us, I need to be just me, just

Alexis who's attracted to you. Who's just a little bit crazy about you. Who wants you more than she wants the next breath of air.

"So *damn it*, Leandro, give me something. Give me something that's free of your manipulation, of your duty, of what you think I need. Give me something of yourself. Or we end before we begin and it's Izzie who'll suffer."

Awash in such pure desire, eddied around by such sharp heat, Leandro was captivated by her. Drank in the unflinching honesty in her eyes, of the way she held his gaze even as her mouth trembled.

And something inside him unraveled at the stark, unabashed courage in her words.

"Pink." The word came out of him as if it was wrenched from the depths of his being, as if it was chipped off a concrete wall around his heart leaving a thundering crack behind.

"Pink?" she said then, frowning, the confidence in her eyes flickering.

He couldn't take it anymore. He couldn't stand that feeling of being ripped open with his emotions bare. He needed her taste, her scent to wash away that feeling of being stripped of his control.

So he took her mouth with a voracious greed, with little finesse. His teeth scraped against her lips as he forced her to open to him. Just as he had forced her to accept him into her life.

If there was a different way, Leandro admitted, with a sinking feeling, he didn't know how.

But Alexis opened her mouth, *Dio mio*, it was pure heaven.

Nothing existed but the sweetness of her mouth, the current of need building up inside him. The press and fit of their bodies as if they were designed for each other.

Even the thought of his friends and family seeing him

like this, undisciplined and hungry for a woman, didn't stall his raking hunger.

She fisted his shirt in her hands, her soft groan music to his famished senses. "Leandro, no, tell me—"

He tugged her lower lip with his teeth and growled. "I bought this cursed dress because it was pink. Because I remember your fixation with everything pink. Because I knew you would like it. Because I wanted the sheer pleasure of seeing you in it, because I wanted to see your pleasure in it.

"I saw it almost a month ago in a catalog on my desk, before you even came back into my life and thought of you. And this past week, I couldn't stop thinking about it, so like a schoolboy who wants to impress the girl he likes, I hunted it down to the designer store. I explained to them what it looked like, I described your size and I waited for two hours while they flew it down here from a different store in Rome.

"I have never, in my life, gone to such lengths to buy a small thing like that.

"Is that bit of madness enough for you, Alexis?"

And because he couldn't bear to see his own reflection in her eyes, because he couldn't pretend like he hadn't heard the desperation in his voice, he turned away.

Still, she stopped him. Kissed his cheek boldly. Demanded that he hold her gaze. "*Grazie*, Leandro," she said, warmth in her tone.

Why couldn't she fight him and call him a hateful man for manipulating her, for taking advantage of her situation? What courage did she possess to give of herself this way, to wrench parts of him he didn't want to give?

Such joy glittered in that brown gaze that for the first time in his life, Leandro felt truly out of his element. Her taste on his lips, her scent on his skin, that curve of her mouth, the warmth in her gaze, suddenly they were the most terrifying things he had ever beheld. Because they were both a tremendous gift and an almost unbearable burden.

For he knew now that he wasn't enough to hold those intact, knew how easily he could shatter it *and her* and then…and then he had a feeling his entire world would collapse along with it.

And he wanted neither this power nor this vulnerability that Alexis brought into his life.

CHAPTER NINE

ALEXIS'S HEART POUNDED, every sense felt amplified a thousand times as she paced the length of her room.

She hadn't been this anxious even seven years ago when she'd been naive and Leandro had been the reckless fantasy she'd indulged in.

He was still an unattainable fantasy come true but now she understood the man, what made him so irresistible to her and even better, she understood herself.

All through the long, unendurable evening, she'd been aware of Leandro's every word, every movement, of the possessive light in his gaze and his touch. It was as if there was a current that tugged and tossed them even with other people around.

And, yet, somehow, he had also been her anchor in a sea of unfamiliarity.

Every time someone had blatantly wondered at how she'd landed his interest despite her lack of high connections or illustrious career, he'd batted them away with that arrogance. Threw out casually that it was his stars that had aligned finally that Alexis had come back into his life.

That moment had stretched infinitely, Alex's heart in her throat at the genuine sentiment in his words.

Soon, with Tina's help, Alex had separated the covetous from the caring ones, the superficial hangers-on from sure but curious friends of the family. And if Tina was distracted, there was Luca.

Tears had filled her eyes at how his family soon embraced her, and Alex knew it was from Leandro that they took their cue.

So strange that she'd received what she had always craved for, from the man who manipulated her into accepting it.

Now, it was past midnight and Izzie was out for the night after thoroughly enjoying being the center of attention. And she knew Leandro would be here any second.

She had all but issued an invitation. But acting the confident aggressor who wouldn't back down was easy when it was all words and safe kisses. When they were surrounded by a hundred other people.

Now, now she trod a path on the thick carpet, her nerves stretched to the hilt. She was wondering if she should just change into her pajamas and wait for him or remain in her dress and brazenly go to him when she heard the door open.

Nape prickling, chest tight with ache, she turned.

Leandro stood leaning against the door just like he had that first night. His jacket was discarded, hair rumpled. But this time, there was no fury, no distrust, no inscrutability. There was only a fire and she knew he was going to set her aflame tonight, demand everything she had to give, bend her will to his.

Just because she'd demanded he give her a tiny part of him.

"Am I allowed in here, Alexis?" Stark longing pinched those features, making him look sharper, harsher. "Have I paid the toll to be in your room?"

She stared at him, heart in her throat. A dangerous light glinted in his eyes as he pushed off the door. Tension swathed the room. "Toll, Leandro?" Unease fluttered through her gut, knotting it until fierce anger came to her aid. "Is that how you still see this? After everything I've said to you, will you still call this some sort of trade between us?"

He shrugged and approached her, something predatory in his very gait. "I'm trying to understand if I've paid enough to touch you, to be inside you."

Alex wanted to howl and rage and scratch that arrogance off his face. Wanted to throw those hurtful words back at him. She wanted to take Izzie and walk right out of his life. She wanted to—

No, she wouldn't give up this easily. There had been such vulnerability, such desperation in his tone when he had told her about that dress. She pressed her hand to her stomach, felt the silk under her hand and slowly, a thread of her courage, her determination returned.

He couldn't stand needing her like this, couldn't bear that she'd ripped that invulnerability he believed he possessed. So she played his game and dared him. "I want this as much as you do."

His head jerked toward her, his gaze drinking her in. "Izzie won't wake up again tonight, will she?"

Without waiting for her answer, he crossed to the connecting door, looked through it and then locked it.

The sound of the latch clicking magnified in the fraught silence. Turning around, he undid the cuffs of his shirt and pushed them back. Long fingers moved to the buttons on his white shirt then. With a casualness that only betrayed his need to be in control, he unbuttoned it all the way, pulled it out of his trousers and shrugged it off.

Alexis's pulse raced, pounded.

The shirt slithered to the ground soundlessly while moonlight bathed olive-gold skin stretched taut over contoured muscles. A smattering of hair covered his chest, a line of it disappearing down his taut abdomen. Her chest fell and rose at the evidence of his arousal.

Possessiveness streamed through Alex. She wanted to touch him and stroke him and see more of what he hid beneath that facade. She wanted all of Leandro.

"Come here then, *cara*." He pushed off the door and her entire body vibrated as if in tune to him. "Let us see how good our understanding is with each other, how many liberties you'll allow me before you stop me."

"Do you think you can scare me away with those words?" He was the only man she'd ever wanted this intimate pleasure with. The only one who'd made her believe she was bold enough, worthy enough for everything. "You think this is a punishment?"

He reached her and pulled her to him. Pressed a kiss to the back of her hand. His tongue flicked the veins on her wrist. Waves of heat engulfed her as he trailed that wicked mouth up her arm.

Everywhere he touched, pleasure burst forth.

He was as much as prisoner to this fire between them as she was.

Like a mass of clay waiting to be molded by a master sculptor, she went willingly into his hands, gave herself over with complete trust.

"You're a little scared, *tesoro*. Admit it."

She laughed as he turned her around. "No, Leandro. I trust you implicitly."

She heard his heated hiss before he licked the sensitive curve of her neck.

Her knees bumped the high bed and to her back stood Leandro. Their bare feet touched, the buckle of his belt dug into her backbone. His wide shoulders framed hers. Every inch of his rock-hard body imprinted against her shuddering muscles.

Hands on her hips, he kneaded her muscles, stroked them up and down her sides, grazing the sides of her breasts with his palms. Currents swept downward as her nipples tightened, turned into knots of need with a direct connection to the pulse between her legs.

But he didn't touch her where she wanted even as his mouth kissed her back, licking and nipping.

She arched and slammed back into him as his teeth dug into a spot on her shoulder. His erection nestled against her buttocks and lengthened, erotic heat spewing into her muscles. Alex burned to the tips of her fingers, wanting to touch that rigid length.

Her mouth dried with anticipation, of feeling that velvet heat pound through her aching sex.

She heard his curse and rough rasp in Italian when she ground herself against him wantonly. There was no fear when it was this man. No shame in this need that only he fueled within her.

"Should I take you like this, Alexis?" Something she had never associated with Leandro, a feral rawness, a wild heat reverberated in his voice. "Should I bend you over and sheath myself in you, *cara*? I have fantasized about it, I have spilled into my own hands like a schoolboy imagining you like this, *bella*. Should I possess you like I have never taken another woman? That's what you want of me, *si*?

"You want what I've never given anyone else. You want what I don't have to give."

"Yes. I want your darkest fantasy, Leandro."

Reaching behind, Alex plunged her hands in his hair. Reduced the distance between them even more. Her breasts pouted in the air, desperate for his touch. "So stop testing me and tormenting yourself, Leandro."

Her heart pounded in utter contrast to the insouciance in her tone. To take her like that, he meant to deny her the pleasure of touching him, the pleasure of making love to him. He meant to strip this intimacy of tenderness. But if this was what he needed to learn that she wouldn't break, then so be it. "Whatever you want, do it soon. It's been seven long years since anyone touched me. Seven years since I've known this pleasure…and God, I need it more than I need air right now."

Sulky and demanding and utterly sensuous, she couldn't believe that was her.

But unlike him, Alexis reveled in the current that thrummed through her, in this feeling of being so sharply attuned to another person.

"You have not been with another man." His shock and disbelief coated the air.

"I've never wanted another man like I want you. Then or now," she said simply. "Do you still not get it, Leandro? You make me want to risk everything. You make me want to live."

Something reverent fell from his lips as he held her tight against him.

She felt the breezy air from the windows on her puckering nipples and bare flesh before she heard the rip of the silk. "Wait, no…" she cried but already the silk was pooling at her feet.

Breath crashing over her, she shuddered, told herself it didn't matter. The dress might be beyond repair but what it represented was enough for her.

One finger traced the ridge of her spine as he whispered at her ears. "I will buy you a thousand dresses, Alexis," gravel-rough, his voice was a sultry caress just on its own, "and then rip them all off you. By the time I'm through with you, you won't even think of another man, much less ask him to put his hands on you."

With that heated promise, he moved his hands around and cupped her breasts. Rough and abrasive, the sensation was beyond erotic. Alex moaned and pushed herself into those hands. His fingers pinched the needy nubs, sending arrows of wet heat to her sex. "Please…" she moaned, trying to turn in his arms, needing more desperately. Thighs trembled, knees shook as his touch became rougher, her nipples turning into turgid points of pleasure and pain.

But he didn't let her turn. "Please what... Alexis? Should I stop? Is this too much for you to bear?"

"Not enough," she groaned. For the life of her, she couldn't stop begging.

"Should I take these lovely breasts in my mouth, *cara*? Should I tangle my tongue on these tight buds and suckle? Should I use my teeth on them?"

"Yes, please, God, yes," she muttered, quaking from head to toe.

"Maybe if you please me, *bella*," he offered, his words full of retribution and Alex wanted to kill him right there.

He moved his hand down the concave plane of her stomach, pushed his fingers into her thong. Deliberate and torturous, he traced the crease of her folds with exquisite pressure.

Breath was fire in her throat. "Damn it, Leandro... Will you kill me?"

His delicious laughter played along her very nerves. And then he flicked the swollen bundle screaming for his attention.

Alex jerked as he rubbed it between his forefinger and thumb, a groan clawing its way out of her throat. Fever took over her lower body and she rocked herself against his fingers instinctively.

Threw her head back against him and whimpered as pleasure edged closer but still remained elusive.

"Widen your legs for me, *bella*," he commanded.

Thighs trembling, she did.

She had no mind of her own, no will of her own. She would have gone down on her knees and tasted him if he willed it of her in that moment.

Her thong out of the way, his fingers found her aching sex again. "*Dio*, you're so wet for me. So hot for me. Raise your knee," he asked again and when she did, he plunged first one and then another finger into her wet core.

His other hand stroked her bare buttocks, moved up and down her spine.

Fire. Need. Desire. She had everything and nothing.

Alex became a mass of a million different sensations as he stroked in and out and his thumb pressed on her clitoris.

Fine droplets of sweat beaded all over, her own skin was a prison. Whorls of pleasure gathered in momentum and intensity, threatening to break her into a thousand pieces if relief didn't come soon. The world narrowed to her sensitive flesh and his fingers and the blinding pleasure of both.

Throat dried. Nerves screamed.

"Come for me, *mia cara*," he persuaded her, rough and husky and bit down on her shoulder.

Tension corkscrewed through her belly and tightened and tightened until her climax beat down on her in relentless waves. Alex threw her head back against his shoulder and let out a deep keening cry that sounded erotic to her own ears. Her pelvic muscles contracted, released, spasmed, still his fingers stroked her. On and on it went until she didn't know where or what she was. Until she was only fragments of sensation and pleasure.

She fell against him, only upright because he was holding her.

His hands moved the damp swathe of her hair from her neck and he flicked her skin with his tongue, whispering soothing words as if she was a distraught filly. "*Dio*, you come like thunder streaks the sky, you taste like lightning in the air..." She felt his shudder at her back, the rigid press of his erection against her butt. "I never stood a chance against you, *bella*."

The desperate hunger in his tone woke Alex from the stupor of her pleasure.

Determined to have whatever he gave her, swallowing

down her self-consciousness, Alex anchored herself on the arm around her midriff, and started to bend forward.

Instantly, he stiffened around her, stopping her from moving. "Leandro?"

Whatever his dark threat, whatever he'd forced himself to say, to consider, whatever strategy he employed to keep Alexis in her place and his roiling emotions in theirs, Leandro knew he failed.

That she'd undone him.

He already felt as if he'd cheated himself of the sight of her unraveling, of seeing those gorgeous eyes widen and flash in pleasure, of that sensuous mouth softening. Of being drenched in the passion of her cry.

So before the tremors of her orgasm had subsided, even before she had caught her breath, he turned her around, desperate to see her.

She hung on to him like a limpid doll, eyelids drooping down, pink flush staining her cheeks and damp neck, her naked body bowed in the aftermath of her release.

High and pouty, her breasts were a languid invitation, the flare of her hips, the lithe length of her thighs a sensual feast.

Desire and tenderness and every emotion he'd never experienced buffeted him from all sides. How had he even assumed he could separate sex and emotion, especially when it was Alexis?

How could he be in control when she eroded it so easily? How could he hold himself back when she stole all of him by giving everything of hers?

Hands on her hips, he lifted her onto the bed. He shed his trousers and boxers and climbed up over her.

Feasted his gaze all over her damp, trembling body.

Doe-like eyes fluttered open and then widened slightly. "I can see you," she said with a smile. "And touch you. I've had dreamed so many times of stroking my hands over you, of learning every inch of you. Of seeing your eyes widen in desperate need. Of you smiling at me, of knowing that you revel in this attraction between us as much as I do."

"I do, *bella*," he admitted hoarsely. He bent his head and surrendered to this woman. "Touch me, Alexis. All you want."

Pushing herself onto her elbow, she reached out instantly. Fingers fell on his shoulders and fluttered down his collarbone.

Feather-soft caresses that burned him. Light strokes that learned him.

Traced the ridge of his chest. Moved in maddening circles that made his throat dry.

"Leandro?"

"Si, mia cara?" he said breathless and still beneath her tentative touch, pulse thundering under the surface, senses screaming for more.

A fingernail raked his nipple. His breath hissed out of him. "Why does the press call you a saint?"

"The press is not always truthful, *bella*."

"But they call Luca the devil and I know he is one when he sets his mind to it." Now her finger moved over his abdomen, traced the roped ridge of muscle there and moved lower.

Grasping her wrist, he pushed it up over her head. With her other hand, she smoothed his brow, plunged her hands into his hair and tugged. Mouth against his, she pleaded with her lips.

She didn't demand like he had done, she simply gave of herself. And made him give of himself to her.

"After the night we shared, I stayed away from women for a long time."

"How long?" she whispered, pressing her hot little mouth to his pectorals.

"Does it matter?"

"To me, yes." Now, her tongue came out, licking him as if he was her favorite dessert.

He fisted his hands on the sheets, desire a live beast inside him. "Alexis..." he groaned, and held her hair in a punishing grip.

As if she understood his unspoken command perfectly, as if she was tuned in to every dark fantasy he had ever had of her, she grazed his nipple with her teeth. When she pursed her mouth and sucked on his skin, Leandro jerked, his erection drawing tight against his belly.

Dio, he wanted her on her knees, that pert mouth around his rigid length. He wanted all the pleasures with Alexis that he'd never allowed himself before.

Her mouth reached his abdomen now. Steel would have more give than his muscles then. "Do you still want me to believe I was one of many?" she whispered against his skin. "That I was just a convenient lay?"

"*No*...my father...was indiscriminate with any number of women, abusive of my mother in ways I can't even bear to mention. I promised myself a long time ago that I would never become like him." He forced the words out wondering if they would bring back a little sanity. "After I was with you...that next morning, I realized you had been a virgin. That I had taken you like that, with such little tenderness, against the wall, that even your gasp of pain couldn't penetrate the haze of my desire..."

A hard, inflaming kiss that delivered the depth of her want on his lips. It soothed and yet claimed. "But that pain was momentary, Leandro...nothing compared to what I felt after. Nothing compared to what you made me feel."

He closed his eyes, the memory haunting him even now. "I couldn't bear to look at myself. I couldn't stand to think I had been so reckless with my hunger. So mindless.

"And I abhor befriending women, letting them think I

was interested when I had no intention of ever marrying, just for sex. So I never touched another woman again."

Something akin to wonder crossed her face as she cradled his cheek. "Seven years, Leandro?"

The implicit trust in her gaze, the pure pleasure in the curve of her mouth felt like a gift, one he had never received before. "Any release I needed, my hands provided it."

Even as she stared back at him like a queen, gloriously naked, color suffused her cheeks at that. "Then it's true. I have toppled the saint from his pedestal," she whispered with a satisfied smile before she claimed his mouth.

Soft and tentative, she slanted her lips this way and that, looking for that perfect fit. Swiped her tongue over the seam of his lips.

He pushed his hand through the silky curtain of her hair and held her there, awash in the heated seduction of her mouth. But he needed more. Soon, he took over the kiss. Dueled his tongue with her tentative one. Scraped his teeth across her lush lower lip. Sucked it into his mouth.

He explored and ravaged that soft mouth so thoroughly that her whimper raced along his spine.

But it wasn't enough. *Dio,* nothing was going to be enough except utter possession. And complete surrender.

He pushed her onto her back and covered her body with his. Inch by inch, skin to skin, hardness against soft curves, he settled over her lithe body.

A perfect fit, as if they were made for each other.

As if there was magic in the room. Something beyond passion and pleasure. Beyond the frantic beats of their hearts and the sweat-slicked friction of their skin.

There was a raw intimacy, a closeness with Alexis that he vowed to never lose.

Alex's jagged growl joined his as her breasts rubbed his chest, as she brought her knees up and his thick shaft settled against her womanhood. He jerked at the heated invitation of her sex, slick against his. Her arms vined around his neck, fingers plunging into his hair and scraping. Softness settling against his hardness in all the right ways.

She was made for him, the thought circled him.

"Leandro, please, I want to touch you... I want to—"

"No, *cara*. I can't...wait anymore."

Pushing her thighs wide with his hips, rough hands holding her down for him, he entered her in one slick thrust and sheathed himself in her fully.

A gasp wrenched out of her as her sex stretched and closed over him like a tight fist. Every muscle in him screamed for movement, for friction, sweat gathered on his forehead. Leandro buried his mouth in the crook of her neck and counted his breaths.

Only then did he realize the tension in Alex's body, the punishing grip of her fingers on his shoulders. The thought of hurting her, *again,* cleaved him in two.

"Alexis, *mia cara*," he said, her name a prayer on his lips, "did I hurt you?" Had he been rough in his desperation?

Slowly, she relaxed under him, her breath blowing warmly against his shoulder blades. "No...it just feels unfamiliar and strange."

Her skin tasted like summer to his lips. "Good strange?" he somehow managed through the shrieking demands of his body.

"Overwhelmingly good, achingly...intimate." Her words mirrored his thoughts in a moment of pure perfection. She glanced at him and then away as if she needed to hide her expression from him. "Don't you think so?"

He smiled against her trembling mouth. "You think me capable of thinking, *cara*?"

After a moment, she found his gaze again. Kissed the corner of his mouth.

Slowly, her hands drifted down his back, cupped his buttocks and then she wiggled her hips under him. Liquid fire surged through every nerve ending. "I like when you can't think, Leandro."

It was all the sign he needed.

And then he was thrusting deep and hard inside her, breath balling up in his throat and she met him thrust to thrust, raking her fingers over his back, urging him on and on with her whimpers and moans.

Hands on her hips, he tilted her up for him and pistoned in and out, deeper and faster.

The slap of flesh, the pounding of their hearts, the damp whisper of their skin…

There was nothing civilized, nothing even remotely like self-control left in him anymore. Only the mind-numbing pleasure rushing at him mattered.

In the blink of a breath, he moved his hand and tugged the center of her slick sex with his fingers.

With a whimper, Alex bowed and bucked and fell apart around him and the convulsions of her body sent Leandro careening toward his own release.

Pleasure splintered him into a thousand pieces, slammed his heart awake as if it had merely been a functioning organ until now. His very breath a fire in the back of his throat, Leandro let out a guttural grunt at the surfeit of sensation.

Alex's hands came around him and held him hard as he fell from the dizzying pleasure.

And Leandro knew that he'd never been more vulnerable in his entire life. Knew why he'd fought and resisted this rushing fate from the moment he'd seen her again.

Not when he'd discovered the abuse his father had heaped upon his mother. Not when his mother had walked out and he had hugged a sobbing Luca and had taken on the mantle of his family and business. Not when Rosa had died and he had suddenly felt anchorless.

It seemed as if there were no coping strategies left. No automatic mechanisms that his mind could conjure to lift away the strange weight on his soul, the fever in his blood.

Alexis had burrowed herself under his skin, into his heart and if he lost her, he had a feeling his world was never going to be the same again.

CHAPTER TEN

"ALEXIS?"

Burrowing deeper into the warmth of his body, Alex purred. Or at least that's what the sound that escaped her throat sounded like.

"Wake up, *tesoro.*"

A deep languor claimed every sated muscle, every sensitive nerve ending. Leandro had carried her to the en suite and washed her. A rainfall shower that she hadn't known existed, purple marble tiled bathroom and Leandro's roving hands that had persuaded and pushed her to another release—the erotic sounds from her own mouth were going to haunt her every time she went in there.

Her sex felt swollen and pulsed between her legs, her muscles sore in the most delicious sort of way.

Mind numb with a profound sense of well-being, she took her own time before she remembered he'd said her name. "Hmm?" she answered back lazily, tossing about on the bed.

"Stop wiggling around and stay still." Large hands, capable of heart-wrenching tenderness, gripped her. "I can't think if you keep doing that. Or I can think of only one thing."

As if he didn't trust her to listen, Leandro himself shifted behind her.

His arm went around her waist and rested snug between her breasts, the long T-shirt she'd donned after their shower no barrier. Somehow, she had convinced him she needed the T-shirt, not completely comfortable with her nudity yet.

He was another issue altogether. The rough velvet of his skin was a visual and sensual feast she couldn't get enough of.

As if there was an embedded chip that reacted to his touch, her breasts became heavy, nipples sprang to peaks.

One of his legs rested between her thighs and she could already feel him hardening against her again. Her head rested on his hand, his hands combed through her still damp hair.

Need slowly uncoiled within her again. She traced his leg with her foot, a languid invitation. "Something wrong with that?"

He pushed away her foot and slapped her on her bum. "Behave, *cara*."

She grabbed his hand and pressed a kiss to his rough palm. "Sorry, I forgot, you're ancient and decrepit. This last session probably wiped you out." She made a regretful sound as she moved a palm up and down his forearm. God, how she loved the silky rasp of his hair-roughened arm against hers. "I won't see action again for a while, will I?"

The words had barely left her mouth when he pushed up her T-shirt, lifted her leg and entered her from behind.

The shock of his invasion made the pleasure sharper and a desperate cry wrenched from the depths of her soul. She clutched his forearm and hitched out a hard breath.

"Any complaints now, *cara*?" he asked at her ear, his breath a rattling rumble.

"God, no," Alex whimpered as he tested their fit. The sensation was exquisite, like a lick of fire traversed down her spine, lighting every nerve ending on fire.

He felt even deeper like this, as though he was a part of her that she never wanted to lose.

"Take off your T-shirt," he growled then. With arms

that could barely hold up, Alex managed to roll the thin cotton up and over her head.

The moment she did, he slid his hand under her head, turned her so that her torso faced him. "One more time, *mia cara.*" Dark and deep, his command sent shivers through her.

Alex groaned, every inch of her supersensitive. "Enough, Leandro, please."

He shook his head, his fingers rubbing her lower lip. When he pushed his finger into her mouth, she sucked on it. Wet heat rushed between her legs, and she writhed restlessly against him.

The dark sensuality of his demands was as revealing of the man as they were of her.

Such passion he leashed, such need he'd denied for so long, Alexis couldn't help but feel as if only she had unlocked it. Only she that all his desires belonged to.

Only she that could make all his fantasies come true.

"Yes, *mia cara.* I need to hear your scream, again." His eyes with a deeply possessive heat. "It's never going to be enough with you, *bella.*"

- Her gaze collided with his, excitement and something else a pulsating drum in her ears.

Without breaking her gaze, he bent that dark, arrogant head and took her nipple in his mouth. Soft lips suckled in that persistent rhythm that he'd discovered she liked until a flood of fire filled every inch of her.

And then he was moving within her even as his teeth grazed the hard knot, their flesh more joined than even before.

Control and inhibitions were dust beneath the thunderous roar of pleasure and the darkly sensual net of intimacy. They danced to a primal, age-old rhythm, instincts already honed to each other's needs and wants, hearts pounding together, skin slicked with sweat.

Release came upon them together in a violent cacophony of such pleasure that Alex thought she had died under the onslaught of it and became born again anew in Leandro's arms.

After what felt like an eternity of heaven, Leandro spoke into the darkness. The sheets were blissfully cool against her skin. And behind her, Leandro a fortress of warmth.

"Tell me about these folders that are full of drawings and stories."

Alex stiffened, hitched a much-needed breath. She clicked on the night lamp and turned toward him. "How do you know about that?" She sounded defensive, but she didn't care. "It was horrible of Antonio to snoop into my private matters. For you to do that is just plain crossing so many bloody lines. Don't manipulate me—"

"Izzie told me."

She tried to move away from him but his grip only tightened. "Because you prodded her?" she snarled. "Will you use her now to get your way?"

"*No.* She sounded very upset that she found you crying over one of them when you thought she was sleeping."

"Oh…" Dismay and a sense of failure swirled through Alex. "I should've been more careful. I hadn't realized… God, she must have been so scared. What did—?"

"Shh…calm down, *tesoro.* Izzie is just like you, strong and resilient. I reassured her that I would take care of her *mamma.*"

The wild beat of her heart calmed as Alex glanced into Leandro's gray eyes. She bit back the instant, defensive retort that sprang to her lips. It was his instinct to be protective, true. It didn't mean that he didn't care for her, just a little.

She couldn't believe him heartless anymore, not after

what they had shared. Not now when she understood what had made him so rigidly protective of those around him.

Something in her ached at the thought of him losing his innocence at such a young age, of him taking over responsibility for Luca and Valentina.

How would there be anything left for his own indulgence? Would he even know his own heart when it had always been buried under such weight?

"Thanks for reassuring her," she said.

Something warm filtered through his gray eyes and he laced their fingers together. "Should I thank you for raising such a wonderfully strong girl? We're a team now, *si*?"

She nodded, liking the sound of that.

The kiss he pressed to the back of her hand was tender, almost reverent. "So…what do I have to do to have the privilege of seeing the contents of these folders?"

"How do you know it's a privilege?" she retorted, keeping it casual.

Sharing those stories was like giving him a piece of her heart, the most precious, guarded part. So much of her sense of self was tied to them.

What if he thought they were rubbish like her parents had done? Or what if he used them and their value to her to manipulate her?

Alex didn't think she could bear it if he did that. There would be no coming back from that, even for Izzie's sake. It was better to keep that part to herself as she'd always done.

That way lay safety. For all of them.

"Izzie says they are fantastic. I believe her."

"Izzie is six years old. And they are very private. Only one person's seen them besides Izzie."

Instantly, he scowled. "Justin?"

Alex smothered a smile, knowing it would only rile him further. He sounded so fiercely jealous and her heart did a skip. *God*, how pathetic was she. "No, Adrian," she answered. "My parents thought it was an utter waste of time when I showed them once."

"Your parents are idiots, *bella.*"

"Hey!" She swatted him on his shoulder. "I'd just gotten an F in math, they discovered Adrian pretty much did my science project from start to finish *and* they had been called to a meeting with the teacher to discuss my lack of *application to academics.* And then they found out I had pages and pages of these…doodles," Alex repeated her mother's word, though a part of her still hurt at the denigration. "They didn't know what to do with me."

"So tell me, what did Adrian think of them?"

How did he always know to ask the right question?

"He loved them and told me I should never stop. Never lose my pleasure in them. He had all these grand plans of becoming my agent and selling them and used to beg if he could live off me when I became a famed, big-name author." Tears filled her eyes, just remembering his goofy smile and his tight hugs. And his easy acceptance of all her flaws and weird quirks. "He was just being kind but I loved him even more for that."

"Wait, so other than Adrian, you've never shared them with anyone? Never wondered if they should be shared with people, if they would bring pleasure and joy to someone else?"

Alex shrugged. "I told you they're not important."

"Leave it to me to decide that," he growled back at her. In utter contrast, he cupped her cheek with such tenderness and kissed her mouth. "Why were you crying, *bella*?"

She lowered her eyes, her insecurities and her love of those drawings roping together into a twisted knot. "I was just probably feeling emotional. You already know that the accident was bad and not just physically."

"Will you lie after telling me we have to do better with each other, Alexis?"

Alex sighed and pulled up her left hand. She could never share them with him but maybe speaking of her loss would lessen the pain of it?

"I'm left-handed, Leandro. For years, those drawings and stories were my only escape, my only relief from the pressure I felt at not being brilliant like Adrian. Even from the grief of losing him.

"Now, I can't even hold a pencil properly for more than a minute, much less draw anything. It feels like the one thing I enjoy so much—" The one thing she thought defined her, the one thing she had built her entire identity around, "—has been snatched away from me."

As if she was now truly nothing, just as her mother had said for all those years.

Her tears slipped from her eyes, and Alex hid her face in his neck, refusing to let him see them.

She felt so small in that moment, like that little girl who had forever waited for her parents to tell her that she was loved just as she was.

But at least now, she had accepted that no one would. That her own acceptance of herself had to be enough. There was relief, painful but still there, in that truth.

Soundlessly, he wrapped those corded arms of his around her and squeezed her tight. "We'll see world-class specialists, *cara*. We'll do whatever it takes. It'll come back, you will see. Whatever exercises they prescribe, you'll do them with me from now on." Authority clipped his words, making it a harsh command. "No more lifting things or—"

Instantly, her hackles rose. "I'm not an imbecile, Leandro. I've been doing everything I was told to."

"You will indulge me. In the meanwhile, you can show me some of those lovely folders, *si*?" Pure mischief glinted in the gray eyes and the serious mouth, transforming his entire face. He looked younger, carefree in a way she'd never seen him. "I think it's important to share them with me so that you don't feel like you're alone—"

Alex thumped him hard on his shoulder. "You're a horrible, manipulative man, do you know that? You just can't help it, can you?"

Laughing, he fell back against the bed, and took her with him. Alex lay sprawled over him, her legs tangled with his, her breasts crushed against his muscles. It felt so natural to lie with him like this, so effortlessly easy.

"Maybe I'll have to withhold other things from you until you share them with me then."

Share them with me...

He was asking to know a part of her, showing interest in the thing that mattered to no one except her. Only Adrian had ever done that.

A matter, for all Leandro knew, that didn't give him any advantage in this relationship of theirs. Hope yawned in her entire being, an incandescent flicker that was as good as imagining that she, only Alexis, and not the idea of the mother of his child, held his interest now, without his sense of duty chaining him to her.

"Let's see about that," Alex challenged before sliding over him and straddling him.

She gasped as she felt him hardening and lengthening against her core, just where she needed. She fisted her hand around the base, and the feral growl that fell from his mouth filled her with a satisfaction unlike she had ever known.

Rising up on her knees, she took him into her body and then there were no challenges between them, no withholding, nothing but mutual pleasure.

Alex finished her swim in the infinity pool and rubbed down her arms and legs. The Italian sun was at its peak but she lingered at the covered stone patio deck for another few minutes.

The scent of olive trees and the spice garden to the side of the villa that she had learned Leandro tended to personally permeated the air.

Among all of Leandro's estates and she had toured a mind-gaping number of them this past week with him and Izzie, she liked Villa de Conti the best.

And not just because of the spectacular view Lake Como offered either. There was a peace, a kind of quiet here in the villa that she didn't see elsewhere. A sense of happiness among the three siblings, of what they had built together after the disastrous, it seemed, almost destructive consequences of their parents' marriage.

Even as Valentina sometimes rebelled at his dictates and Luca, quite recklessly, provoked Leandro, just for the fun of it—the devil—over the past few weeks Alex had realized any happiness they had found, the love they shared was because of Leandro.

In the name of duty he did it, but the fact that he would give anything for their happiness warmed Alex's heart.

Also, Valentina lived here and they had become fast friends again. Even Luca dropped by every few days and somehow Alex felt as if she was as much a part of their family now as Izzie was.

Or perhaps it was the absence of Leandro's grandfather, Antonio.

The old man hadn't said one word to her again, hadn't even approached her. Only looked at her with a cutting hostility but Alex told herself she didn't need his approval.

She knew, however, that Antonio was still a large part of Leandro's life. He seemed to be the closest to a friend and mentor Leandro had. But something about him didn't sit well with Alex.

She hoped it was just her reaction to the old man not liking her and making it very obvious.

Grabbing a robe from the lounger, Alex pulled it on and

headed for her bedroom. Izzie was out with Valentina and the afternoon stretched ahead of her.

Alex showered and dressed.

Settling in the shade in the sun-drenched terrace, she dialed her parents' home number, eager to hear how their trip went. When an automated voice told her that the line was disconnected, she called her mom's cell instead.

It took her mom barely five minutes to cut across Alex's questions and blurt out her excitement.

Her parents had sold the store to an interested buyer who had offered them loads of money for the prime location.

Alex made all the necessary comments, faked excitement she didn't feel.

How many times had she tried to get a refinance for their house with the store as a guarantee? And yet someone had spent a bucketload of money on it.

But the weight on her chest refused to melt away as she went through the day. Something about her parents' sudden bout of good fortune made her uneasy.

Or was it just her attachment to the store, she doubted herself again. Was it just that things were changing too rapidly for her peace of mind or was it something else?

Days passed by in a blur as Alex tried to hold on to the wave of change that rocked through her life.

Only nights spent between the sheets with Leandro made her feel together again. Only by laying against his warm chest and hard body could she retain a sense of herself, could hold the reins of her life.

Outside of it, the weight returned to her chest.

Her parents' selling the store.

Valentina not only meeting the enigmatic Kairos Constantinou, but within three weeks of meeting her, Kairos proposing marriage to her.

The rapid-fire argument she had caught between Leandro and Luca over Kairos.

That vague sense of unease returned a hundredfold and Alex struggled with it for days.

It felt like a dark portent, like a choice was rushing at her that she didn't want to make. As if the sense of well-being and wonder she had discovered with Leandro would be ripped away at any moment.

The sounds of revelry from the gardens that floated up through the windows and the balconies, of snippets of Italian and Greek, of the sultry jazz tune that Kairos and Valentina were dancing to, the intensely lush colors of the summer—jasmine and rose, and the scent of wild orchids that decorated each table...

Everything faded as Leandro straightened from the vanity sink and his gaze fell on the wrapper half peeking out of the wastebasket.

He'd almost missed it and if not for the word flashing at him like a neon sign he would have thought nothing of it.

Half of that phrase winked at him as if playing peeka-boo with his already somber mood.

Fingers turning as cold as the gold-tinted marble, he stared at it. It seemed as if he was being petrified from the inside out, such was the stillness inside him.

He didn't know how long he stood like that, looking at it, but unmoving. And then shattering that stillness, laying waste to that stony silence inside him came a howl from his throat that should have quaked the very foundation of the centuries-old villa he stood in.

It propelled him into action, and he bent his knees, and pulled out the wrapper gingerly, as if it was a bomb that could detonate at any moment and decimate his suddenly fragile life.

Breath ballooned up in his chest, crushing his lungs as he read the script on the wrapper.

Someone had taken a pregnancy test.

And since this was Alexis's bedroom, the bedroom in which he had made love to her in the past six weeks, he had little doubt who. He had forgotten to use protection that first night after the party.

And after that, Alexis had told him they would have to use condoms until she went back on the pill.

He had bitten off his retort countless times about how they wouldn't need it if they just got married, like he wanted to.

Her mouth falling open, she had looked at him in disbelief. "Married? You want more kids?" she had said, as if the very prospect was scary.

"*Si.* Where did you think this is leading?" he'd thrown back at her curtly, frustration turning his temper ragged.

"Marriage is a big step," she'd countered then. "And I can't even think about more kids now."

He'd barely held back the snarl that rose to his lips. "You would have us continue in this vein, sneaking into bed at night and into closets during the day? For how many days do you think you can fool Isabella?"

For how many more days would she torture him this way?

For days, there had been a compulsion in his blood, a pulsing throb under his skin that he needed to secure their future. That he needed to bind Alexis to him in any way he could.

But she had told him not to rush her, that she was enjoying their learning each other, enjoying the freedom of being his lover without the restrictions and confines of marriage.

Maledizione! He should have dragged her to the church by the hair after that statement.

But no!

Vulnerable in a way he'd never been before, having no experience of this confusion within, he had let her set the tone for their relationship.

After all, he'd manipulated her thoroughly, hadn't he?

It was the only thing she'd ever asked of him. That they take it slow.

He understood the word *sucker* that Luca used for some of his friends.

He had thought to make her happy, to gain her trust. He'd taken her to the opera and when she had challenged him, he'd watched a marathon of some cult TV show because she'd called him a traditional, stick-up-his-ass, starchy brute.

He made love to her in the night in her room, like some illicit lover, because she insisted on not confusing their daughter before matters were settled between them.

Dio, she hadn't even come into his room once. Hadn't let him take her in his bed. She didn't let him wake up with her in the morning, shuffling him out of her room at dawn because she thought Izzie would wander in.

And now to find this…

The test, where was the test…he went to his knees. With shaking fingers, he upended the basket.

Maybe it wasn't positive, the vulnerable, emotionally weak part of him piped up. *Maybe that's why she hadn't even mentioned it. Maybe he was making a big issue out of—*

And the plastic, rectangular tube lay faceup on the white marble, the answer winking up at him.

She was pregnant!

Alexis was pregnant. With his child. Again.

And she hadn't told him.

Cold chill infiltrated Leandro's skin, clamped his very bones.

She hadn't said a word all day.

He had seen her at the lavish breakfast he had arranged in Kairos and Valentina's honor just for family. She had sat next to him, a little bit lost, until Luca had prodded her.

He did that always, Leandro had realized irritably. Made Alexis smile and laugh. Looked after her in a way he'd never seen Luca do before with another woman.

After the breakfast, they had both gone their separate ways, a hundred things on his mind about the engagement party tonight.

Until he had come upon her, here in this bedroom and asked her point-blank if something was bothering her. If there was something he could fix for her.

She had fed him a white lie that she was anxious about her dad's health.

Too afraid to examine his own spiraling anxiety about her continued refusal, he had accepted her answer.

Had made love to her in that very bed while the entirety of his family and three hundred members of Italian society had been arriving on his estate. Stroked and tasted and touched every inch of her until his name was a litany on her lips.

Because only there could he strip her defenses, only when she was naked and writhing beneath him, only when he drove away everything else with his hands and mouth and touch, did Alexis belong to him completely, mind, body and soul.

All last week, she had been curt, a little distracted, even with Izzie. Even Valentina, as self-involved as she'd been, had commented on Alex's appetite.

Which meant Alexis had known, or at least guessed, the truth before this morning.

With a growl, he pushed away the basket, threw the test on the floor.

Hurt and pain were like twin spikes in his sides, stealing his very rationality. Shredding that sense of control he had always needed to handle his world.

Why hide the truth from him this time? What did she fear? Or had she decided she didn't want to be with him after all?

I would like to visit New York for a couple of weeks, she had said just yesterday, throwing him for a loop.

Why? Why go to New York now?

Why was she pulling away from him?

And what could he do to stop her?

CHAPTER ELEVEN

IT WAS ALMOST dawn and she still hadn't come to him, still hadn't told him. And for the first time since that night when he had made love to her, Leandro kept himself away from her bedroom.

The party had come to an end hours ago and the dense silence, the pitch-dark of the night, suited his somber mood. Somehow, he'd held on to his control. His jaw should have turned to concrete hours ago for the way he'd gritted his teeth and greeted everyone.

His face should have turned to brittle glass for the happiness and normalcy he'd had to fake.

His blood should have chilled to ice at the sight of Alexis in a navy blue silk dress that hugged her curves so gloriously. She had looked strained though he was the only one who noticed.

Like him, she hadn't wanted to mar the happiness of Valentina's big night.

If he went to her, he would weaken.

If he touched her, if he lost himself in the sensuality of her body, he wouldn't care about why she was avoiding him.

If he took her and moved inside her, the hurt wouldn't lessen when he was done.

Because he would still be outside of the wall she'd erected between them.

It was nothing but a madness and Leandro was through with being this mad, this out of control.

He had to do something to shred this fear. He had to take action.

Only action, only setting things right had always saved him. Had stopped him from crumbling. Had enabled him to take care of Luca and Valentina.

And the right thing was that Alexis belonged with him just as Isabella did.

She was his and he wouldn't let her go.

He reached his study and slammed the door shut behind him.

Countless times, he had come in here, to swallow his tears. To bury his fears. To shore up his courage so that he could act like an adult when he had barely been one.

Here was where he had lost his innocence and discovered that the man who should have protected them all was an animal instead.

Here was where he had threatened Enzo after he had raised his hand at their mother.

Here was where he had hugged Luca when they'd discovered the horrible truth their mother swallowed.

Here was where he had argued with Antonio, for days, about the rightness of bringing Valentina home.

A growl rumbled through him at the thought of losing Alexis, too.

He had just poured a generous measure of whiskey, something else he'd never indulged in as a rule, when the door opened behind him.

Even in that moment, his breath hitched in his throat, hope flared.

Antonio stood at the door and Leandro turned away from his grandfather's shrewd gaze. He didn't want anyone to see him like this.

Not when he didn't understand himself.

"Drinking, Leandro?" Antonio's challenge was instant,

dry and carried the weight of a thousand questions. Enzo had not only been an alcoholic but an abusive one.

All of them, even Antonio, had felt the effects of that.

Leandro threw back the whiskey in a reckless gesture. It seemed he was finally coming apart at the seams and he hadn't even realized that he had been holding so tight. That his complacency and his control were this flimsy.

The fiery slide of the whiskey against his throat and chest blunted the edge of his roiling emotions. Just. He faced Antonio and shrugged. "Maybe I have earned the right, Nonno?"

Antonio's cane was a harsh rap against the gleaming marble floor. "Maybe you have become weak."

Leandro remained silent, hating to agree with Antonio.

"That woman, what has she done now?"

Brittle laughter escaped Leandro's mouth. Apparently, the only absolute in his shifting world was Antonio's black prejudice of Alexis.

"She is pregnant."

A fierce kind of joy lit up Antonio's old eyes, so raw that Leandro looked away. He thumped Leandro on the shoulder, the force of it no less for his frail body.

"Marry her soon," he declared as if that hadn't been a foregone conclusion from the moment Leandro had seen that Alexis needed him just as much as Isabella did.

Why couldn't she accept it when Leandro offered her everything?

"The Conti heir cannot be a *bastardo*—"

"You do not know if it is a boy, Nonno, and she has not told me."

Antonio missed a beat. "You think she will use this to manipulate you?"

"Alexis doesn't have a manipulative bone in her body."

"Then why does it—" Antonio stared at Leandro, then

frowned as if he couldn't fathom the import of this. "This matters to you? That she has not informed you?"

Leandro drove his shaking fingers through his hair. Trust his grandfather to arrive at the crux of it so easily. "*Si*, it does. It means I still do not have her trust. It means she still has not accepted that we must marry."

It means that he still did not have her heart. And that clawed through him.

Something dawned in Antonio's gaze. Whatever it was, Leandro didn't like it one bit. "She leads you by your manhood, she refuses to marry you and now...she plays with your emotions. I knew this would happen."

Running a shaking hand over his nape, Leandro bit back his stinging retort.

The sounds of a file slapping the mahogany desk brought his head up.

A grim sort of triumph danced in Antonio's eyes.

"What is that?" Leandro inquired.

"Read it for yourself."

A small insignia on the top right corner of the file was Leandro's first clue—a highly expensive Milanese private investigations firm.

A passport-size picture of Alexis, maybe eight or nine years old, that naive but defiant tilt to her chin, his second clue.

Pages and pages of information on Alexis from school grades to jobs, including the time she and her friends had received a mark on their juvenile record for some minor shoplifting. When she had been fired from a job at an accounting firm when she'd been eighteen—the year after her brother's death, he remembered.

Facts even he didn't know about her pregnancy. The loan on her store that had been almost defaulted. And then details about the accident and her recovery.

Nausea barreled up Leandro's chest and filled his throat.

"What in hell is this?" The question was rhetorical yet he couldn't wrap his mind around it.

"It's a report that I had that firm put together a week after that woman stormed into our home. That shoplifting record, those bad investments, and this accident recently... it is not a hard story to put together.

"I can find a lawyer in two minutes who will label her an incompetent mother. And your children will be yours."

"I will not separate my children from their mother. I need her in my life, Antonio."

Leandro's stark statement echoed around them while Antonio's mouth tightened. But he did not care. *Dio*, he did not care about anything.

For the first time in his life, he wanted, *no, desperately needed*, something to even go on. He wanted Alexis's heart, he wanted to be loved by this strong woman, he wanted to bask in the generosity of her laughter and passion. He wanted to go to bed with her through countless dark nights and wake up with her to a million sunrises. He wanted to help her heal and see her soar...

Yet he did not know how to keep her from slipping away from him.

She was. *Dio, she was.*

"I could not hurt her with this, Nonno. I could not forgive myself if I hurt her."

"Then use it in my name. Use it to scare her, use it to bind her to you."

Leandro jerked away from the table.

It was so diabolical and yet simple.

Antonio could force her hand with this very file. Even a whisper of a separation from Isabella would send Alexis into his arms. Leandro could reassure her it was not true, but persuade her to the altar with him. And she would be Leandro's forever.

Once Alexis gave her commitment, once she vowed

herself to him in marriage, there would be no going back, whatever way she'd arrived there.

She would be that perfect, adoring wife, her loyalty toward him and their family absolute. He knew that as well as he knew his own mind.

A life with Alexis and Isabella and his unborn child, just as it should be, versus this anxiety, this confusion about her feelings, this desperate chasm that he couldn't fill no matter what he did.

If he used it, Alexis would be shattered. It was the worst thing he could aim at her, even in the guise of Antonio, the worst that she believed of herself.

But if he didn't...what if she never agreed to marry him? What if after everything Leandro had done, he wasn't enough?

He could have the only woman he'd ever wanted in his life this badly.

What, per carita, was he waiting for?

Alex felt every passing second like a net was drawing in closer around her. Soon it would choke her if she didn't tell Leandro about the pregnancy. The terrifying anxiety she had felt at seeing the test positive had calmed now, but not the fear of the oncoming fate.

She hated cheating him of this news every passing second, especially as she knew how elated he would be.

A big, loving family, he wanted it. He wanted everything he and Luca and Valentina hadn't had growing up. He would shower this baby with just as much love as he did Isabella. He had so much love to give, and yet, would he open himself up to feeling anything remotely like that for Alex herself?

Again and again, he talked of duty, of what an exceptional mother she was, of giving Isabella security, of the rightness of all of them together...

And nothing about her and him…

Nothing about why he wanted her with a desperate intensity every night, about the raw fear she saw in his eyes when he didn't think she was looking at him, about the urgency and anger she sensed gathering in him every time she postponed their talk of future…

Would he ever learn that he had to risk his heart to have and hold hers? Would it all be her capitulation but none of his? Would he only manipulate her again and again, like he'd already done with her parents' store?

For one question of Luca and five minutes of his time had told her that some offshore branch of Conti Luxury Goods had acquired a tiny health food store in Brooklyn.

Why, why did he need to buy their store and offer that exaggerated price for it?

Was it just to retain control of this situation between them? To arm himself against her?

So every time she had gathered courage yesterday, every time she had firmly put her reasons for not jumping into marriage, fear eroded her courage.

That she would let him persuade her, that he would forever bind her to him without ever opening his heart to her, that she would forever wonder if it was something to do with her that stopped him from loving her… Alex didn't want to live like that.

She didn't want to spend the rest of her life like she'd done for so long. Craving her parents' approval and attention but never receiving it, calling herself inadequate and not being able to help it, forcing herself at things that she'd never been good at and failing…

On and on, the cycle would go on…

God, it would be a thousand times worse with Leandro, for she wanted more from Leandro than she'd ever wanted from anyone else.

She wanted him to want her because he couldn't live

without her. Because he loved her, just as much as she loved him. She wanted him to be desperate for her, just as she was.

Bloodthirsty of her, true, but how could she live with anything else?

When she knew walking away from him would shatter her into a thousand different pieces.

The morning had started out horrible with nausea churning through Alex's stomach. She had barely slept, waiting and wondering if Leandro would come to her.

When somewhere around dawn, she'd realized he wasn't going to, she had cried herself to sleep. The tears felt both like a burden and a relief for she was no closer to deciding what she wanted to do.

She'd desperately wanted to go find him, to sink into his embrace, to tell him how much she loved him. But what would he say? What if he only took advantage of it?

What if he turned the biggest truth of her life into another weakness?

She emptied her glass of orange juice and decided to take Izzie out for a walk when Luca walked onto the terrace, a grim expression on his face.

Fear was a fist in her throat for Alex knew, instantly, that something was very wrong.

Luca threw a file on the table. "I promised I would help." There was no warmth or charm in his tone. A nerve flicked violently in his temple while that laughing mouth set into a hard, cruel curve.

It was such a change in his demeanor that it took her a few seconds to focus on the file.

Like a snake uncoiling, ready to strike and sink poison, it stared back at her. "What is it, Luca?"

"A file, *cara*." His tone tempered and perversely, it

made her throat raw. "About you. To prove that you're an incompetent mother."

Alex jerked so hard that she'd have toppled off the chair if not for Luca's hand behind her. Her heart thumped in her chest, a loud rushing in her ears made her head spin. The nausea she'd felt this morning returned a hundredfold.

She gripped the edge of the breakfast table, looking for an anchor in her drowning world.

Incompetent...the word was a like a burn mark on her skin, festering and deep and painful. More so than all the pain she'd suffered in the accident.

More so than all the years of tears and deprecation and grief she had suffered at her parents' hands.

With shaking hands, she opened the file. Watched pages and pages of her life distilled into hard little facts. Stripped of her insecurities and fears. Reducing her entire life into one dimension.

Disorganized. Years of her chaotic nature, her rebellion against being compared to Adrian's obsessively organized life.

Poor financial straits. Years of having slaved over the store and the house and nothing to show in return. Apparently, no loans at least, thanks to Leandro.

Panic attacks. Incomplete use of one hand.

No career prospects.

Doubt was a pit of thorns that she tumbled into, mocking her, scraping her.

It was every horrible thing her mother had insinuated over the years and every fear she had made herself sick over again and again.

Alexis bent her head to the table, and pulled in a deep breath to keep the grief rising through her at bay.

No, she refused to be reduced, refused to let her pain, her fears, her very life, be reduced to such cold, hard facts.

This wasn't even about her.

She wasn't a failure. Not the woman who took what she wanted seven years ago. Not the woman who had a daughter and raised her against all odds. Not the woman who dared set the rules with a man as ruthless and autocratic as Leandro.

She dashed away the tears before they could spill. Rage was a feral thing inside her and she let it roam freely. She stood up and faced Luca. "Do you know who commissioned this?"

Please, let it not be Leandro, she prayed frantically.

If he'd done this, she could never forgive him. There'd be nothing but ashes left.

"Antonio." Relief battered her. "A chartered flight leaves in three hours. It is best if you take Izzie and leave."

"You think Leandro will use this against me." Horror seeped into her words.

"I have stopped guessing the lengths to which my brother will go to ensure what he thinks is right. He's done it for too long and knows nothing else." The impact of Luca's fist on the table rocked through Alexis. "Maybe I was wrong and there's no hope for—"

A fist to his mouth threw Luca back. Loud and vicious, his pithy curse rent the air. Heart rapping against her rib cage, Alex pushed her chair back and stood up.

Shock buffeted her as she realized it was Leandro that had thrown the punch at Luca.

Knuckles bruised, mouth tightened into a thin line, gray eyes blazing with fury, it was Leandro like she'd never seen before.

When he moved toward a barely upright Luca again, Alex planted herself in front of him. "Stop it, Leandro. What the hell is wrong with you?"

Something swept across Leandro's face then, a black, glittering shadow that sent ripples of alarm up and down her skin. "He not only advises you but aids you to run away, with Isabella in tow, and I should forgive him?"

"He aids me because he has lost hope for you. Because he thinks—" her chest was so tight, "—that you're an unfeeling brute who would manipulate me into spending my life with you without earning it, without even deserving it."

That arrogant head of his reared back as if she had slapped him. That sensuously wicked mouth that had licked and caressed her to rapture flinched. But Alex felt no satisfaction in hurting him, in piercing that steely invulnerability of his.

How could she when her gut was twisted into a painful knot, when her heart thudded in fear of a future that could very well be ruined?

Luca's harsh, pain-filled laughter surrounded them. He stepped forward now, past Alex, as if challenging, almost inviting, Leandro to take another swing at him. "Our parents have ruined him, too, *cara*. You are a fool to trust him."

The contempt in his tone left a jarring reminder even after he left.

A bleakness touched Leandro's gray gaze even as it swept over Alex in that hungry way of his. "Have you decided I do not deserve to know that I'm to be a father again?"

He didn't demand in a fury or betrayal but as if he'd already lost her. As if she'd hurt him immeasurably by not sharing it with him. "It's not something I could hide from you long."

"But you did not share it with me in happiness. That is telling enough."

"I hated not telling you every moment. I hated depriving us of the joy of it…but *God*, Leandro, you manipulate everything around you, arrange everyone's lives." Tears she'd held back fell out of her eyes. "I trusted you, always and you...

"Is he right, Leandro? Would you have used that file against...me?" Her voice broke, throat full of needles. "Did you consider it?"

His strength and heat surrounded her, and Alex almost leaned into him, driven by deep need and instinct. When he spoke, he sounded as if his own throat was full of gravel. "I considered it. For all of five minutes.

"I was desperate, *bella*, I could feel you slipping away from me this past week. And then you wouldn't look me in the eyes, you hide this news from me."

He rubbed the heel of his hand over his eyes, the vulnerability of the gesture tugging at Alex even now.

"Because you made me doubt everything. You bought my parents' store and didn't say a word to me. You talked of marriage and duty and family but not of us. Not once.

"I couldn't live like that again. Not when I discovered how...

"Not for Izzie, not for this baby. I couldn't settle for something less again. Not from you, of all the people in the world. I deserve to spend my life with someone who loves me, Leandro."

"Are you leaving me then, Alexis?"

The stiffness in her spine relented, the rigidness of her muscles melted and Alex struggled to regulate her long exhale.

For in that tiny question, she discovered a universe of meaning.

The old Leandro wouldn't have asked such a desperate question. As if it was all beyond him now. He would have never accepted defeat when he could move mountains and rearrange landscapes for his purpose.

His pain in those words and the relief it provoked was a

tiny, threadbare bridge between the chasm that had opened up between them over the past week.

Hope flickered in her chest.

Heart in throat, every inch of her skin hyper-aware of him, Alex stared back at him. Refused to even betray her heart by the flicker of an eyelid. "If I do take Luca's help and leave, it's your own fault.

"If you lose the right to be Izzie's father, if you lose this joy that we could've had…" she swallowed away the words that rose to her lips, "then it is all your fault.

"It is your own refusal to open up your heart to me, your own stubborn, arrogant belief in thinking you know best, your bloody incapability to feel anything, that would ruin the best thing that's come into your life."

The silence clattered with the beat of some bird's wings across the blue sky, with the soft hum of a lawn mower somewhere, the world puttering on its humdrum way while her heart stuttered in her chest.

"You think me unfeeling, *mia cara*? To attack my own brother like an animal, you think I'm not weak? You think it doesn't terrify me at this moment that there is nothing I can do to stop my very life from falling apart? You think it didn't disgust me that I considered even letting you see that file?

"My heart is not mine anymore.

"My fate is not mine anymore.

"I have been rendered into nothing at your hands, *tesoro*. I'm nothing without your love."

And just like that, the man she loved with every fiber of her being went on his knees.

That stunning, honorable man raised his head toward her and spoke the words she'd been dying to hear with every breath in her. "All my life, I have tried to control and master every emotion. I lived only to make sure no one ever hurt me and Luca and Valentina, without ever risking anything… I didn't even realize what I missed until I met you.

"You…you make me risk everything, *bella*. To place my happiness in your hands, to trust myself into your hands, it terrifies me.

"But I love you so much, *mia cara*. If you give me one chance, I will change. And I will love. And I will risk everything I have again and again to prove I'm worthy of the woman I love more than anything else."

The woman I love more than anything else…

Tears filled and overflowed from Alex's eyes at the pure supplication in Leandro's words.

Her trust in him soared on wings, her entire being felt as if she could float away on a cloud of happiness.

She fell to her knees in front of him and took his mouth with hers. He tasted of passion and thirst and hunger that could never be sated, and of love.

Of unconditional love, of utter acceptance, of deep, abiding trust.

Frantic words in Italian caressed her skin as he pressed kisses to every inch of her face, as he wrapped his strong arms around her and held her tight. His anxiety spoke in his shaking fingers, in his tight grip.

In the shudder that went through him when he said roughly, "*Per piacere, bella,* tell me you're not leaving me. Tell me you'll stay and love me. Tell me you'll let me be a part of your life, *cara*.

"I would take nothing that you do not want to give, Alexis. Never again."

"I love you, Leandro, so much." Alex buried her mouth in his neck, breathed in the taste and scent of him. "I would have killed you if you had used that against me. I'd have—"

"Shh…*mia cara*. They are all lies, you know that, don't you? If anything, I'm the one incompetent to love you. I'm the one who's not worthy of you and Izzie and this baby."

He pulled her to him right there until she sat in the cradle of his thighs, and his hand found her stomach.

"I hate him, Leandro," she said snuggling into his warmth. "I'll never forgive him for putting such idea in your head."

With gentle fingers, he clasped her chin, understanding her. "He's old and set in his ways, *cara*."

Fear made her words sharp, harsh. "What if you had lost me because of his horrible advice? What if we had lost all this?"

"You know what I see when I look at him, Alexis?

"Myself, if you hadn't come along. He has been through grief and loss and such pain to be hardened by it all, *bella*. He tried to do right by Luca and me in his own way.

"If nothing else, I have to keep him around the family as a reminder of what I could become if—"

"You're generous and kind and honorable, Leandro." Alex turned around in his arms and pressed her forehead to his. "You're the man I love. You would never become like that. You could never hurt anyone you love like that."

Her belief in him unmanned Leandro, her love for him shook him. "But I already have, Alexis." A shiver ran through him and Alex turned and embraced him again.

"What do you mean?"

Leandro hid his face in her shoulder, fear fisting his gut. How foolish he had been in thinking he could arrange and assure everyone's happiness around him. When his own wasn't in his hands. "Luca hates me. And Tina... *Dio*, Tina's entire happiness hinges on the fact that the bet I made is right."

"You set up Kairos with her, didn't you?" Alex asked, her perceptive gaze settling on him.

"I did. I couldn't risk Antonio threatening to tell her that she's not a Conti. If she was married, if she wasn't one anymore, I thought she would not care. Luca thinks, rightly, that I have gambled with her happiness.

"If she discovers it, she will never forgive me. And I will lose her."

Alex caressed the clenched muscles in his back, clasped her arms around Leandro tight. She understood Luca's anger now, and the underlying fear. But she couldn't let the man she loved suffer. Pressing her mouth to his temple, she lifted his chin. "You did it with the right intentions. You did it because you love her so much.

"She'll understand one day, Leandro. Because she loves you. Just as I understood what you did with me."

The trust in her eyes, the fierceness of her embrace, Leandro realized for the first time in his life that he wasn't alone anymore. That he didn't have to bear the burden by himself. That Alexis would seek to protect him just as he would do with her.

The depth of her love filled him with a quiet strength. He brushed his lips against hers, sensing a hole he hadn't even known inside fill. "Promise me that you will spend eternity with me."

With a kiss, Alex agreed.

EPILOGUE

Ten Years Later

LEANDRO STOOD LEANING against the wall by the entrance to the small bookstore while cold November rain and sleet pounded the streets of Seattle.

A fire burned brightly in the stone hearth on the far corner, its hissing sparks and flames adding to his wife's spooky storytelling abilities.

His mouth curved as she reached the part where the magical squirrel reached the dark cave she had to venture into.

High and low, deep and bass, she modulated her voice to match the ferocious tiger and the shaking squirrel while the group of children surrounding her wore matching reactions of wonder and shock and anticipation. Some smiled with a knowing look for they knew what came next, some shuddered for they were hearing the story for the first time.

His ten-year-old Violetta and six-year-old Chiara watched Alexis with wide eyes and wider mouths as if they couldn't believe that their *mamma* could be this entertainer extraordinaire who authored such magical, elaborate stories.

It had taken him eighteen torturous, agonizing months to win Alexis's trust, to receive the last piece of her heart, to see the stories she had written and drawn pictures around for so long.

The innocence hidden in the stories despite the treacherous adventures, her particular gift of transforming the average, the downtrodden, the underdog into tremendous heroes meant her success after being published had been meteoric.

And Leandro had cherished every moment of this journey with her, was humbled every day that this brilliant woman was his in every way that mattered.

He wasn't sure Chiara even understood that Alexis was such a famous children's books author.

To her and his other girls, she was just their loving, adorable and, in Izzie's case recently, a little strict *mamma*.

Remembering his teenage troublemaker, Leandro turned. At sixteen, his eldest was already giving him minor heart attacks with her rebellious streak. She hid in one of the back aisles chatting with a boy and throwing him warning glances to not even acknowledge her.

Turning around, Leandro smiled widely.

He wouldn't admit it to her even at the pain of death but he loved Izzie for exactly what she was, even as she drove him up the wall every other day with her tricks. He loved all his girls as different as they were for they were all pieces of his heart.

Something Antonio still couldn't grasp after all these years. Just remembering Antonio's crushing disappointment when Chiara had been born made Leandro chortle even now.

That the Conti male heir he so desperately wanted, that he wanted to groom, was Luca's son was a bitter pill he still couldn't seem to swallow.

He straightened from the door to the sound of thunderous applause from a bunch of tiny hands. Alex stood up from the stool but waited patiently as some kids asked her to sign their books and some just asked about the magical squirrel's next adventure.

Violetta ran toward Izzie and Chiara followed while his wife made her way toward him.

The moment she reached him, Leandro took her mouth in a fast, hard kiss. Cheeks staining pink, Alex pushed at him. "Bookstore, Leandro, and children, remember?"

His hands on her hips, Leandro dragged her to his side and locked her there. It had been three months of Alexis's book tour with his entire family. Of Chiara crashing into their bed because she didn't like her bed, of Isabella hating her life and Violetta following her little sister.

"I can't help it, *mia cara*. It's going to be hell once we get to the hotel again."

Alex elbowed him in the ribs. "You're the one who wanted a big family, remember?"

"Yes, but I thought they would all be saints like me. But they are like you—"

This time, it was she that pressed her mouth to his.

Dio, his hunger for this woman would never abate and he liked it just like that. "Take me home then, won't you, Leandro? To our big bed and endless privacy and to those long nights." Wicked laughter made her eyes shine. "Maybe we can fob them off on their *Zia* and have a fourth honeymoon." She swiped her tongue over his lips in a languid invitation and then drew back. "That is, if you're up to it."

Leandro pressed her hips until she could feel the rigid length of him. "I'm always up for you, *bella*," he said nuzzling her hair.

Pink stained his wife's cheeks, a soft gasp fluttered out and he fell in love just a little more. Every day, he fell a little more, the magic of it filling his every breath.

"I love you, Leandro." She never let him forget it.

Through day and night, joy and sorrow, Alexis never let him forget that he was loved.

"*Ti amo*, Alexis," he whispered back, his heart bursting to full.

* * * * *

Look out for the dramatic conclusion to
THE LEGENDARY CONTI BROTHERS
THE UNWANTED CONTI BRIDE
Available July 2016

In the meantime, don't miss
Lynne Graham's 100th book!
BOUGHT FOR THE GREEK'S REVENGE
Also available this month

MILLS & BOON®
Hardback – June 2016

ROMANCE

Bought for the Greek's Revenge	Lynne Graham
An Heir to Make a Marriage	Abby Green
The Greek's Nine-Month Redemption	Maisey Yates
Expecting a Royal Scandal	Caitlin Crews
Return of the Untamed Billionaire	Carol Marinelli
Signed Over to Santino	Maya Blake
Wedded, Bedded, Betrayed	Michelle Smart
The Surprise Conti Child	Tara Pammi
The Greek's Nine-Month Surprise	Jennifer Faye
A Baby to Save Their Marriage	Scarlet Wilson
Stranded with Her Rescuer	Nikki Logan
Expecting the Fellani Heir	Lucy Gordon
The Prince and the Midwife	Robin Gianna
His Pregnant Sleeping Beauty	Lynne Marshall
One Night, Twin Consequences	Annie O'Neil
Twin Surprise for the Single Doc	Susanne Hampton
The Doctor's Forbidden Fling	Karin Baine
The Army Doc's Secret Wife	Charlotte Hawkes
A Pregnancy Scandal	Kat Cantrell
A Bride for the Boss	Maureen Child

MILLS & BOON®
Large Print – June 2016

ROMANCE

Leonetti's Housekeeper Bride	Lynne Graham
The Surprise De Angelis Baby	Cathy Williams
Castelli's Virgin Widow	Caitlin Crews
The Consequence He Must Claim	Dani Collins
Helios Crowns His Mistress	Michelle Smart
Illicit Night with the Greek	Susanna Carr
The Sheikh's Pregnant Prisoner	Tara Pammi
Saved by the CEO	Barbara Wallace
Pregnant with a Royal Baby!	Susan Meier
A Deal to Mend Their Marriage	Michelle Douglas
Swept into the Rich Man's World	Katrina Cudmore

HISTORICAL

Marriage Made in Rebellion	Sophia James
A Too Convenient Marriage	Georgie Lee
Redemption of the Rake	Elizabeth Beacon
Saving Marina	Lauri Robinson
The Notorious Countess	Liz Tyner

MEDICAL

Playboy Doc's Mistletoe Kiss	Tina Beckett
Her Doctor's Christmas Proposal	Louisa George
From Christmas to Forever?	Marion Lennox
A Mummy to Make Christmas	Susanne Hampton
Miracle Under the Mistletoe	Jennifer Taylor
His Christmas Bride-to-Be	Abigail Gordon

MILLS & BOON®
Hardback – July 2016

ROMANCE

MILLS & BOON®
Large Print – July 2016

ROMANCE

The Italian's Ruthless Seduction	Miranda Lee
Awakened by Her Desert Captor	Abby Green
A Forbidden Temptation	Anne Mather
A Vow to Secure His Legacy	Annie West
Carrying the King's Pride	Jennifer Hayward
Bound to the Tuscan Billionaire	Susan Stephens
Required to Wear the Tycoon's Ring	Maggie Cox
The Greek's Ready-Made Wife	Jennifer Faye
Crown Prince's Chosen Bride	Kandy Shepherd
Billionaire, Boss...Bridegroom?	Kate Hardy
Married for Their Miracle Baby	Soraya Lane

HISTORICAL

The Secrets of Wiscombe Chase	Christine Merrill
Rake Most Likely to Sin	Bronwyn Scott
An Earl in Want of a Wife	Laura Martin
The Highlander's Runaway Bride	Terri Brisbln
Lord Crayle's Secret World	Lara Temple

MEDICAL

A Daddy for Baby Zoe?	Fiona Lowe
A Love Against All Odds	Emily Forbes
Her Playboy's Proposal	Kate Hardy
One Night...with Her Boss	Annie O'Neil
A Mother for His Adopted Son	Lynne Marshall
A Kiss to Change Her Life	Karin Baine